"Tracy Richardson has created an intriguing premise that blends the worlds of sci-fi, spiritualism, and climate activism."

—ALLEN JOHNSON
Screenwriter, *The Freemason*

"An ode to the responsibility of taking care of our one and only Earth, *Catalyst* offers an energetic and immersive experience that spotlights alternate dimensions, energy fields, and our very own human potential."

—GENESE DAVIS
Game Writer, Author of The Holder's Dominion series

"*Catalyst* frames a portrait of collective humanity for each of us to find our likenesses rendered within a profile of the human condition."

—RITA KOHN
Senior Writer for the NUVO Cultural Foundation

CATALYST

CATALYST

TRACY RICHARDSON

BROWN BOOKS
PUBLISHING GROUP

Catalyst

Brown Books Publishing Group
16250 Knoll Trail Drive, Suite 205
Dallas, Texas 75248
www.BrownBooks.com
(972) 381-0009

A New Era in Publishing®

Publisher's Cataloging-In-Publication Data

Names: Richardson, Tracy, author.
Title: Catalyst / Tracy Richardson.
Description: Dallas, Texas : Brown Books Publishing
    Group, [2020] | Series: [Catalysts] ; [2]
Identifiers: ISBN 9781612544458
Subjects: LCSH: Excavations (Archaeology)--Fiction. | Mothers
    and daughters--Fiction. | Archaeologists--Fiction. | Energy--
    Fiction. | Survival--Fiction. | LCGFT: Paranormal fiction.
Classification: LCC PS3618.I3454 C38 2020 | DDC 813/.6--dc23

ISBN 978-1-61254-445-8
LCCN 2019918840

Printed in the United States
10 9 8 7 6 5 4 3 2 1

For more information or to contact the author, please go to www.TracyRichardsonAuthor.com.

Dedicated to everyone who is waking up to the importance of taking care of our beautiful planet Earth. There is no second planet.

We're made of star stuff.
We are a way for the cosmos to know itself.

—Carl Sagan

1

I'VE HAD GLIMPSES of something beyond my five senses. Usually they're in the form of premonitions and intuition, but four years ago when I was in middle school I communicated with the spirit of a Native American girl. I want to experience that kind of connection again, but I don't know how. Sometimes she inhabits my dreams, and I get up in the morning wishing I could connect with her while I'm awake and wondering if I imagined it all in the first place. It feels like a door that was once open to me is now shut and I don't have the key. Thinking about how she was able to communicate with me without words through time and space gives me a vague, unsettled feeling, as if something is missing from my life.

I give myself a mental shake and pull the door handle to get out of the car, determined not to give in to anxious thoughts. Hopefully the next few weeks will keep my mind occupied with other things.

We arrive at the Angel Mounds archaeological dig site in time for dinner. That's when all the students involved in the field study are supposed to arrive for orientation and a "meet-and-greet evening," as my mom refers to it. It's her dig. She's an archaeologist at the university and I've visited several of her sites over the years, but this is my first time actually working on one. Not bad for a summer job—at least that's what I'm hoping; the work is unpaid, but it's still great experience. She was able to get all three of us—me, Eric, and his girlfriend, Renee—spots on the dig team.

I'm checking out the people milling around the clearing when I see them. Their presence immediately commands my attention. Most of the others are probably archaeology or anthropology students doing a summer field study course, but these two are different.

The man turns suddenly and looks me straight in the eye. It's as if he sensed me looking at him . . . or *thinking* about him. That's how it feels, like he's reaching out and touching my thoughts. I hear him say, *Hello, Marcie*, not audibly, but inside my mind. I take a slight step back, startled, but hold his gaze and the connection between us. In my previous encounters I've never heard words spoken, just experienced thoughts and feelings. He inclines his head toward me and touches the brim of his hat before returning to his conversation with his companion. I'm a little disturbed by the whole exchange. Something about him makes me uneasy. My skin shivers, and I rub my arms to dispel the feeling. Who is this guy, and how is he communicating with me?

I shift my gaze to the woman. Her caramel-colored hair is braided into a heavy rope hanging down her back, and she's gesturing in smooth, fluid motions as she talks. She gives the impression of being both still and animated, reminding me of a cat stalking its prey, immobile save for the twitching of its tail. *Contained* is the word that comes to mind. The way her eyes roam over the other waiting people, stopping only briefly to rest on me, enhances the feline resemblance.

The two of them are standing off to one side of the shelter with their heads together, deep in conversation. Both are holding clipboards and are dressed like everyone else in shorts and T-shirts, beat-up boots and hats. The guy has his back to me, talking to the girl—woman, as they are obviously older than the others, probably graduate students. His hair is black and smooth, held back by a leather tie. It isn't that they look any different from anyone else. They *feel* different. They have a palpable energy about them.

If the woman senses me looking at her, she doesn't give any outward indication, but somehow she seems as aware of me as I am of her. As I'm thinking about this, she steps forward, the man following behind her.

The woman smiles broadly when she stops in front of the three of us, her boots crunching on the gravel underfoot, and extends her hand. "You must be Marcie and Eric, Dr. Horton's children."

"Yes, that's right. And this is my girlfriend, Renee," Eric says.

I take the woman's hand. The connection of our skin—hers cool and smooth, mine probably hot and sweaty—is electric. She tells me that she is very glad to meet me, but not with words. Just like what happened with the man, we're communicating with our thoughts.

"I'm Lorraine, and this is Zeke," she says aloud, waving a hand toward the dark-haired man. "We're senior graduate assistants on the dig. Welcome to Angel Mounds. We're really looking forward to working with you." Zeke reaches out his hand to shake mine, and I look into his arresting gray-blue eyes. I stare at him a moment and stop shaking his hand. He gives my hand a little squeeze and then tugs his away. I recover myself, but the whole encounter has unnerved me.

When Zeke shakes Eric's hand, I realize that he's very tall—taller than Eric, who's well over six feet. They're both tall. Lorraine has to be at least five foot ten.

He puts his hand on Eric's shoulder. "We're very glad you're here. You have important work to do."

At the dig? He seems to be implying something more, but what?

"We're going to let everyone get squared away with their things inside and then meet up at the shelter for dinner and the bonfire," Lorraine says. "Marcie and Renee, you can follow me. Eric, you go with Zeke." She turns toward the old farmhouse that will serve as the girls' dorm.

I grab my suitcase, duffel bag, and tackle box of dig supplies and follow her with Renee, wondering what the summer will be like with these two mysterious graduate students.

2

"WHAT'S KEEPING ERIC?" Renee asks.

We're helping ourselves to the food laid out on one of the picnic tables in the shelter. Her hair swings forward as she leans over to fill her plate, and she tucks it behind one ear. Renee's pale skin contrasts starkly with her dark hair and bright eyes. My strawberry-blond hair and freckles make me feel about as all-American as you can get.

"Who knows." I'm just glad that I'm not the one having to wait for him. I like to be on time, or early, for that matter, and Eric always cuts it to the last moment. "He'll probably get here just as they start the meeting."

"Yes, I bet you're right," Renee sighs, but she's smiling. "Ah, here he comes." Eric is standing in the doorway to the boys' dorm looking bleary-eyed, like he just woke up.

"It looks like he may have taken a nap." I'm not a napper and don't really get how people can go to sleep so quickly. Eric could lay down on one of the picnic tables and fall asleep within moments.

All of the students and staff are gathering in the shelter for dinner. The clearing surrounding the shelter and firepit is flanked on two sides by the old farmhouse and the square, nondescript boys' dorm. The graduate students and faculty are staying in another building in the woods a short distance away.

My mom and the other archaeologist on the dig arrive and call for everyone's attention.

"Welcome to the Angel Mounds site, everyone." My mom is wearing the ubiquitous shorts, T-shirt, and boots. Her strawberry-blond hair is pulled back in a ponytail. I definitely take after my mom in the looks department.

"We're glad to have you all here, and I'm sure you're excited to get started. Please get your food and gather around for our first meeting. I'm Dr. Horton, and this is Dr. Fraser." She indicates the other professor, a man in his thirties or forties—I can never tell. He has a medium build and thinning red hair and is wearing sandals. "Hopefully you all did your homework and reviewed the prework materials we gave you, so my intro will just be a summary." She smiles as the group murmurs affirmative sounds. My mom has everyone's attention and is very much in charge.

A bubbling sense of pride wells up inside me. *That's my mom!* It's not often that I get to see my mom as anything other than my parent. It's easy to forget that she has a life separate from me. She walks around the shelter making eye contact with each of the students and generally putting people at ease.

"You should all have received your room assignments and gotten the lay of the land in the dorms. The graduate students and Dr. Fraser and I will be in the faculty building that is closer to the visitor center. You'll all be on your own here at night, and with that freedom comes the expectation that you won't abuse it." She pauses for emphasis. "That doesn't mean that you can't have fun, but please keep it reasonable. I'm not here to be your mom." I hold my breath, but thankfully she doesn't look at me or make some joke about that.

"As you know, this dig has been underway for the past three years. We're studying a mound-building settlement of Native Americans known as Mississippians who lived here from AD 1000 to as late as AD 1450. The term Mississippian refers to an indigenous culture or way of life that developed in the Mississippi River Valley sometime around AD 800 and grew to encompass the southeastern United States all the way to the Atlantic and Gulf Coasts. For this field study, we'll be excavating a section of the village surrounding Angel and Emerald Mounds and looking for dwelling and meeting structures and storage buildings as well as the artifacts associated with them." She checks her notes.

"I'll give you just a little review of what we know about the site. We call the Angel Mound site the City of the Sun as the largest mound, Angel Mound, is aligned with the movement of the sun—the solstices and equinoxes—and artifacts found there suggest that the chief or head shaman was known as the Sun Priest. The smaller mound, Emerald Mound, is known as the Site of the Moon as it is oriented with the movements of the moon and other nocturnal celestial objects. These people, while primitive by modern technological standards, were very advanced in their knowledge of the movement of the heavens."

She checks her papers again. "OK, let's get started with the team assignments. We have three teams. Team A is led by Zeke and Lorraine." My mom gestures toward them.

Lorraine nods and Zeke tips his hat in acknowledgment as they step closer to my mom and Dr. Fraser.

Lorraine had shown Renee and me our room in the farmhouse and helped us get settled in. It's an old house and the rooms aren't big; our room has just enough space for two bunk beds and two desks. Two other girls, Lainey and Nora, are rooming with us. I'm glad Renee and I are together.

I find myself staring openly at Zeke and Lorraine as my mom talks. There is something mesmerizing about them, and I felt this even more strongly when we were alone with Lorraine in the farmhouse. As if sensing my stare now, she looks over at me and smiles. The warmth of her smile envelops me, making me catch my breath, and I automatically give her a big smile in return. She and Zeke have a quiet presence about them, like they know more than they are letting on.

My mom is still speaking. "Team A members, when I call your name, please come over and join your leaders."

I hold my breath because I feel like I know what's coming next. "Marcie Horton, Eric Horton, Renee Auberge, Lainey Hernandez, Scott Bergman, and Leo Stamatakis. You are on Team A."

Somehow it makes perfect sense that the three of us are on the team with Zeke and Lorraine. We walk over to join them and meet the others on our team. My mom is calling out the rest of the teams, but I've stopped paying attention.

"Hello again." Lorraine's manner is friendly, but her amber eyes are intense and penetrating.

We introduce ourselves to the others in our group. Lainey is curvy with long, dark hair pulled into a messy bun, twinkling brown eyes, and café au lait skin. Scott is tall and lanky with sandy blond hair. They're both from Kansas.

"Greek?" Eric asks Leo. Not only his name but his Mediterranean coloring gives him away.

"Um, yeah." He runs a hand over his dark, wavy hair. "What was your first clue? Stamatakis? I know, it's kind of a cliché: the Greek guy is an archaeologist. My grandparents are from Greece, but I was born here."

"Nice to meet you," I say. "Are you a student at the university?"

"Yup, I'll be a sophomore this fall. I think I'm rooming with you," he says to Eric.

"What about all of you, what's your story? Any relation to Professor Horton?" Leo lifts one eyebrow as if to say, *See, I can play the name game too.*

"Yeah, you got us. She's our mom—Marcie and me, that is," Eric says. "I'm hoping this gig beats a summer job working construction." He indicates Renee and me. "Marcie is my sister, and this is my girlfriend, Renee. You've been lumped in with the whole Horton crew," he tells Leo.

"So are you all archaeology students too?" Leo asks. "Cause that would be a little weird."

"No, just getting the family discount, I guess. Renee and I start college in the fall and Marcie will be a junior in high school."

"Huh." Leo glances toward me.

I don't have time to wonder what that was supposed to mean as Zeke is signaling for us to join him and Lorraine.

"Since we'll all be working together closely and some of you already know each other, I thought we'd start by teaming you up with people you didn't come with as an ice breaker." Zeke's voice is low and resonant.

Renee and Eric exchange a look.

"I know it may not be what you had in mind, but we'll be switching partners a lot, so we'll all get a chance to work together." He quirks his mouth into a smile. "At least I didn't make everyone go around the circle and introduce themselves." He consults a list on his clipboard.

"We'll start tomorrow with Eric, Lainey, and Scott on my team and Marcie, Renee, and Leo with Lorraine. Meet out here by the shelter at 7:45 in the morning and we'll go together to the dig site. Bring your tools. So have fun tonight, but don't stay up too late. We want everyone ready to start tomorrow. Questions, anyone?"

I shake my head and no one else speaks up.

"All right then. We'll see you in the morning." He and Lorraine move off together toward the outskirts of the group around the firepit and disappear into the night.

It's a little before ten o'clock when Renee and I get back to our room. We hung around the campfire for a while talking and getting to know Leo, Lainey, and Scott. Leo lives in Virginia. He came to the university because its anthropology and archaeology departments are so well respected. Lainey and Scott both go to the University of Kansas and are here on a cooperative with Indiana University. They were pretty much in awe of my mom when she came over to talk to us and see how we were settling in, which I thought was hilarious but also pretty cool.

In our room, I start to unpack my suitcase but find I can't finish. The unwelcome anxiety is back now that there's nothing to distract me. I want to talk to Renee about it before Lainey and Nora get back. She has her back to me and is changing into her nightshirt.

"Did you notice anything strange or different about Zeke and Lorraine?" I ask her.

"I mean, they're a little intense, but no more so than the scientists who work in my dad's physics lab. What do you mean?" She turns toward me as she settles the shirt around her hips.

"I don't know. I was getting weird vibes from them, I guess. It was probably just my overactive imagination." I shrug. "Forget it."

I decide to ask her about the other thing that's been bothering me. She and Eric have been helping her dad with some of his experiments on remote viewing of—and connecting to—the Universal Energy Field. Hopefully she'll understand.

"Do you ever wonder if there's more to life, or to the world, than what we do and see every day? Like maybe there's something bigger out there, and if we could only figure out how to connect to it . . . it would be amazing?"

"Bigger? You mean like God, or some higher force?"

"Yeah, I guess something like that. But more tangible, that you can actually experience on a personal level." Now that I've started, I might as well continue. "Sometimes I get these feelings or premonitions that seem like the barest glimpses of what's really out there beyond our five senses."

Renee nods, so I keep talking. "One summer four years ago, at my grandparents' lake house, I communicated with the spirit of a Native American girl. I saw her in visions and in my dreams."

Renee's just listening, not having any reaction one way or the other.

I swallow and continue. "She helped me save an old growth forest from development. It was incredible, but nothing like that has happened to me since. But sometimes I still get . . . hints and vague feelings or intuitions."

Renee has a thoughtful look on her face as she comes to sit beside me on the bed. "I wonder about stuff like that too." She pulls her knees up under her T-shirt. "It's easier for me because of my dad. He thinks the energy fields and the collective consciousness he's studying may be related to a higher power. We talk about it a lot."

"It helps to know I'm not the only one who wonders about this stuff," I tell her, which is only partially true. I still feel a sense of longing to connect with something bigger than myself. I just don't know what it is.

"I think everyone wonders about it to a certain extent. Maybe not as much as you or my dad, though."

I told her I haven't had these feelings in a while, but it's not entirely true. Something about Zeke and Lorraine has my sixth sense on high alert. With them on the dig, things could prove to be very interesting.

3

I'M OUTSIDE BY the shelter well before 7:30 with my tackle box of supplies in tow. The others come out alone and in pairs; Eric brings up the rear right at 7:45. I can't help giving him a look. He always waits till the last moment.

Right . . . on . . . time, he mouths to me as he joins Renee and slips his arm through hers.

I just roll my eyes.

This morning Lorraine seems to be the one in charge. She steps forward. "We're all here now, so follow me to the site." She continues to talk over her shoulder as we follow her along a path leading away from the clearing with the two dorms. "We're going to be working near the larger of the two mounds, Angel Mound."

We pass through a small wooded area and then out into a huge field of tall, waving grass with a large grass-covered mound at the center. A smaller mound is located across the field by a line of trees that run along the bank of the Ohio River, which I know from looking at my mom's map of the site. Several paths like the one we are on have been mown into the tall grass, and the tan clay soil beneath my feet has been packed hard by multiple visitors to the historic site.

"This is so exciting!" Renee says ahead of me. "To see the artifacts of an ancient civilization and try to piece together the puzzle of their existence—it's so fascinating. You know, a lot of what we'll find is the pottery—the art—they created." In the fall she'll be studying graphic design and painting at a university in France, as her family will be returning there after her father's two-year sabbatical at Indiana University is over at the end of the summer. She speaks fluent English, but with a lovely French lilt to her voice, and many of her phrases and mannerisms reflect her Gallic background. As an artist, she really does it all: painting, drawing, textiles (sewing and weaving), and especially pottery. Even with my limited artistic ability I can see her work is good.

"Yeah, I'm looking forward to it too," I tell Renee, buoyed up by her obvious joy in the moment.

We've come up to Angel Mound and are following the path around to the far side. A backhoe and pickup truck with a trailer are parked to one side of a raw, newly dug rectangle about the size of a basketball court. The dirt is covered in plastic tarps weighted down every few yards with sandbags.

"The backhoe we hired has finished taking off the top few feet of soil, so for the next couple of days we'll be using hand hoes and shovels to remove the next layer more gently." Lorraine stops at the edge of the rectangle and the six of us gather around her and Zeke. "The hoes and shovels are in the trailer over behind Professor Fraser's truck. We'll have a short meeting and go over the supplies you should have in your tackle box, then you'll get started."

All of the students cluster around the back of the trailer, waiting in line to get their digging tools. Inside the trailer a fine layer of dirt covers every surface, and plastic bins of shovels and garden hoes line the walls. I grab what I need and go back to the spot where my team is setting up. Everyone has their tackle boxes open, and Lorraine and Zeke are checking to see that we've got everything we need. The day is already getting warm and I take off my hat and wipe my forehead with my bandana. They sent us a packing list, so I would hope everyone came prepared, but I guess you can't be sure. I know I have the all-important trowel and the file for sharpening the trowel, as well as metric measuring tapes and rulers, pens and pencils, and gloves. We were also encouraged to bring a bandana, hat, sunscreen, and water bottle. Of course my mom made sure that Eric, Renee, and I had everything we'd need.

"OK, everyone looks good," Lorraine says once she and Zeke have checked all our gear.

The six of us are sitting or squatting in a semicircle around the two graduate students.

"Over the next few days you'll be gradually removing layers of dirt to get down to the artifact level," Lorraine says. "Even though we don't expect to find much in these layers, there could be artifacts, and you'll need to be observant. You also may begin to uncover the remains of the building structures. We'll be working within the site grid system and screening all the dirt we collect. The entire site is cordoned off into quadrants, and Dr. Horton has the master map of the site. You'll be working in square meter sections to start and placing all of the dirt you remove into your plastic bucket to be screened."

Zeke rises up off his haunches. "My team will start on hoeing, and Lorraine's group will do screening. We'll switch after lunch. Eric, Lainey, and Scott, you can come with me to set up your quadrants, but first we all need to remove the tarps."

We haul the sandbags to the side and stack them, then roll up the tarp to reveal the damp clay beneath. There's going to be a lot of digging in the dirt—and hopefully some interesting finds interspersed.

"This is a way better job than hoeing," Leo says after Scott brings another bucketful of dirt to the raised screen Leo and I are working on. He says it loud enough for Scott to hear and winks at me, so I'm pretty sure he said it just to piss off Scott.

Scott straightens his back. "Oh, you'll get your chance. Don't worry."

I do like the screening work, though. When a member of the digging team fills up his bucket with dirt from the site, they bring it over to us so we can sift it through a screen set up waist high like a tabletop. The openings in the screen are about a centimeter wide, and we work the dirt through it to see if any artifacts are left behind. It's methodical and a little meditative, except that I'm very conscious of Leo working on the other side of the screen from me. He's attractive, with his Mediterranean coloring and lean build, and he seems like a really nice guy too. But I'm also conscious of something else, some other kind of presence around us.

"So you're in high school?" he asks.

"Yeah, I'll be a junior next year."

"That makes you, what, sixteen, seventeen, maybe?"

I'm hoping he's only making conversation and not deciding that I'm just a kid.

"Seventeen. What about you? How old are you?" I already know he'll be a sophomore next year.

"Nineteen." He rubs his wrist against his cheek and leaves a smudge of dirt behind. By now I've figured out that I'm going to be covered with dirt for the next six weeks.

As we work at sifting through the dirt, I'm getting impressions of the people who lived and worked here. Images flash in my mind of men carving tools, women tanning hides or weaving, and children playing games, and even little snatches of conversations float into my thoughts, as if it's happening right now instead of hundreds of years ago. I have a sense of what they think and feel how they live. As though time doesn't exist. I'm so immersed in these imaginations they feel as though they're actually real. Leo's shout startles me out of my reverie.

"Look, I think I found something!" he says.

I come around to his side to see. Leo removes his gloves and brushes the dirt off a small triangular object with his long, tapered fingers. I reach over to take it, and my hand brushes his. I get a *zing* of energy up my arm and jerk my hand away. Did Leo feel it too? I look up at him and meet his eyes. His brow furrows momentarily, then a slow smile spreads across his face. I can hold his gaze for only a moment before looking away. The feeling is too intense. But what, exactly, am I feeling?

"It looks like a piece of pottery," I say, and the moment passes quickly.

"I found the first artifact! Scott will be pissed that it was in his quadrant and he didn't see it," Leo says with a smirk.

There's definitely some healthy competition going on between those two.

"Congratulations," I say, which seems odd, but appropriate. "I think we should call Lorraine over."

Lorraine and Renee have been working together at the other screening table a few feet away. Every now and then someone has to shovel up and remove the dirt from underneath the tables. Lorraine just took a wheelbarrow over to the side of the site to dump the accumulated dirt, and she's trundling back toward us now.

"Lorraine!" Leo holds the pottery shard in the air. "I think I found something."

Both Lorraine and Renee come over to take a look. Leo hands her the artifact.

"Yes, you certainly did." She puts a hand on his shoulder. "This will give us an opportunity to talk about bagging and cataloguing procedures. Whose quadrant is it from?"

"Scott's," Leo and I say together.

"Renee, would you please go over and let Scott know that something was found in his quadrant and to stop excavating? We can take a break and talk about cataloguing."

Renee leaves to go over to the digging team, and Lorraine turns to me. "Marcie, you feel them, don't you? Just like your Indian summer at the lake."

"Uh, yes. How did you know?" I stammer. I'd just attributed it to my imagination, but maybe I really am connecting with the Native people who inhabited this space. Or at least they're communicating with me somehow and I'm picking it up. Or could it be their residual energy still occupies this space and I can connect to it? I don't really know.

"Trust your intuition." Lorraine looks deeply into my eyes. "You are connecting with more than you realize." She turns and walks toward the digging team, leaving Leo and me standing there—with him staring at me.

He bumps his elbow against my arm. "What was that about?"

"Ah, you know, just imagining the people who left these things behind. No big deal."

I'm not about to tell him that I'd been having flashes of Native spirits in my mind, seeing them go about the everyday chores of their lives, or that I'd had a similar experience years ago at my grandparents' lake house. The real question, though, is how did Lorraine know? And what did she mean when she said I'm connecting with more than I realize?

And if that isn't enough, what's going on between me and Leo? Because I feel something there, at least for me.

We hike back to the picnic shelter by the dorms, where its roof and the leafy canopy from the surrounding trees provide welcome relief from the sun. Lunch is leftovers from last night's cookout with cold cuts instead of hamburgers and hotdogs. Eric, Renee, and I are sitting at a table with my mom when Scott joins us and plops a newspaper down on the table in front of us.

"Have you guys heard about this?" He points to the headline. "I went out for coffee this morning and saw it. I don't live around here, but I thought those of you who do might be interested."

The headline reads UNITED ENERGY PLANS FRACKING FOR SOUTHERN INDIANA.

"Wow, fracking," I say. "Isn't that when they pump water and all sorts of chemicals into natural gas and oil wells to extract more gas?"

"Yup," Scott replies. "They've been doing it a lot in Kansas, where I'm from, and it's created all kinds of problems. The methane gas released by fracking contaminates the well water. People I know can actually light the water coming from their tap on fire." He sits down on the bench next to my mom and rests his elbows on the picnic table.

"No shit?" Eric asks. He must've forgotten that our mom is sitting across from him. She raises her eyebrows.

"Yeah, and that's not even the worst of it. The chemicals they use are totally unregulated, so they're basically pumping poison into the rock that leaks into the aquifers deep underground."

"Let me see that." My mom reaches for the paper.

"Here you go, Dr. Horton." Scott hands it over. "I didn't get a chance to read the article yet."

As my mom scans the article, I say to Scott, "You seem to know a lot about fracking."

Scott pushes his sandy blond hair out of his eyes. "Unfortunately, I do. My family farms wheat and soybeans in Kansas, and it's been a big issue for us. The oil and gas companies offer some pretty attractive payments to farmers for letting them set up a well on your land, but they don't tell you about the downside of having all those chemicals surrounding your home and in your water."

"It says they're planning to use hydraulic fracturing technology to extract greater amounts of gas from existing wells in the New Albany shale field in southern Indiana." My mom's forehead is creased with lines of concern. She drums her fingers on the table. "United Energy is offering residents and farmers rental fees for expanding existing wells and drilling new wells on their property."

Leo has come up behind my mom and is reading over her shoulder. His wavy brown hair is damp with sweat.

"Hey, that's great," he says. "My dad says fracking for natural gas is really helping to get us away from relying on oil from the Middle East. Should be good economically for Indiana too."

"We were just talking about how it pollutes the air and water with the fracking chemicals." I meet his eye.

"I don't think there's any proof of that." He shrugs and looks away. "What do the energy companies say?"

"What do you think they're gonna say?" Scott replies. "They say it's safe, of course, because that's in their best interest, but it isn't."

"I'm going to call your dad about this," my mom says to me and Eric as she gets up from the table with the paper in hand. "He'll want to know about it because your grandparents have farmland down here." Wisps of hair have escaped from under her wide-brimmed hat and form a fuzzy halo around her face, but she still manages to look in charge.

"Yeah, you're right."

"Would you tell Dr. Fraser that I might be a little delayed getting back to the site after lunch?" She picks up the bag she uses as a briefcase on the dig and starts walking toward the path leading to the faculty quarters. She already has her cell phone out. Her reaction makes me more than a little concerned.

Apparently Leo didn't want to get into a debate about fracking; he left the table at the same time my mom did. I try to quell my disappointment. How can he be in favor of fracking?

The other people at the table weren't really paying any attention to our conversation, but Renee picks up the thread with Scott. "Did your family allow them to frack on your farm?"

"No, we didn't, but there was a lot a pressure to do it, and ultimately it won't really matter. If the neighboring farmers do it, then the entire aquifer could be contaminated, making all of our wells undrinkable."

"Wow, that's awful." She puts her fork down on her plate. "Is there anything you can do?"

"Some families are trying to get public support against fracking and have legislation passed, but the lure of the rental fees for the farmers and the income for the state make it a pretty hard sell."

"On the drive here we saw small oil pumps in almost every field we passed. There were dozens of them," I say.

"Do you think they'll frack in the Hoosier National Forest?" Renee asks. "The farmland and woods around here are so beautiful. It's terrible."

"I really don't know," I tell her. "I imagine my mom will find out. Then we'll see if there's anything we can do."

4

ON WEDNESDAY A pop-up thunderstorm comes through midafternoon. We all scurry to cover the site with tarps so no artifacts will be lost or damaged and then run for cover back to the dorms in case of lightning. By the time the storm clears, there isn't enough time for it to be worth going back and uncovering everything, so we get a free pass for the rest of the afternoon.

Lorraine pokes her head into the living room of the girls' dorm where Renee and I are hanging out with the other students. "Anyone up for a hike before dinner?"

Several girls groan and say, "No way," but I think a hike will help loosen me up after all the hoeing and screening work.

"Sure!" I swing my legs off the arm of the chair where I'd been reading and turn to Renee. "Do you want to go?"

"How long is the hike?" She's sitting at the table sketching, making use of the art supplies she always has with her. A shaft of sunlight breaks through the clouds outside the window behind her and streams through the panes to illuminate her drawings.

"About an hour to the top where we can rest a while before heading back down. I think you'll like it," Lorraine says.

"Let me text Eric and see what he's doing." Renee already has her phone in her hand and is texting.

"Zeke's over in the guys' dorm asking them now." Lorraine leans against the doorjamb and crosses her arms over her chest. Her thick dark blond hair is loose from its braid now and flows across her shoulders and down her back.

Renee's phone pings. "Eric and Leo are going, but none of the other guys. I guess it's just an abbreviated Team A excursion," she says.

A little surge of happiness blooms in my chest when I hear Leo is coming.

"I guess so," Lorraine replies. "Get some good hiking shoes and a water bottle and meet me outside in a few minutes. We'll take Zeke's SUV to the trailhead."

Zeke's SUV turns out to be a hybrid with lots of seats but not many frills. It does have a good music system, so Eric connects his phone and we listen to music with the windows rolled down on the drive over to Greystone Mountain. The air is fresh with that just-washed feeling it has after a rain and the sun is burning off the clouds. The temperature has cooled down a good fifteen degrees from earlier.

The mountain is part of the rolling hills of southern Indiana that make up the Hoosier National Forest. I wouldn't exactly call them mountains; they're more like large hills. There's a small parking area off the two-lane road. A couple of cars are already parked there, and a path leads into the woods. The path is narrow, so for the most part we go single file. Lorraine and Zeke take the lead. Eric and Renee are behind them, and Leo and I are in the rear. I find it disconcerting to have him behind me. I usually like to be in the back of a group where I can see what everyone else is doing in front of me. It's kind of a control thing, I guess. Also, I keep thinking about him checking out my butt.

"What made you decide to come on the hike?" I ask him over my shoulder.

"I guess you could say I'm the adventurous sort." He laughs. "Seriously, though, I'm always up for any opportunity to get out and explore. The others were mostly glued to some sort of screen."

"That's so true. But I just like being outside." A point in Leo's favor: he's not a slave to his devices or social networking.

I hold a branch high so it doesn't swing back and smack him in the face. He grasps the branch from my hand and lets it snap back into place behind him. His fingers touch mine and I instinctively react by snatching my hand back as though I touched a flame. *Geez. Get ahold of yourself, girlfriend.*

"Your adventurousness should come in handy if you want to be an archaeologist. You'll need to not mind getting dirty. My mom's always in it up to her elbows," I say to cover my extreme reaction.

"Yeah. This dig should be a learning experience in more ways than one."

The hike is gradual but challenging, a constant upward climb. We're all panting with exertion, so conversation stops for a while. The trees all around us have leafed out into a canopy far above, and the vegetation below is composed of low bushes, ferns, and moss on the rocks. I keep my eyes down to watch my feet on the path, but I make sure to look around regularly at the scenery.

We arrive at a ravine with a small creek running through it. On either side are moss-covered rock formations that look like caves carved into the stone. We have to cross the stream on some slippery rocks, so Leo offers to go first and give me a hand across. *He's gallant too,* I think. I'm in favor of women's equality, but to me that doesn't mean ignoring social niceties or not accepting help from guys, so I'm all for that kind of display.

When I make the last jump to the bank, I land a little off balance and fall directly into Leo.

"Hello!" He says as he puts his hands on my hips to steady me.

A hot blush creeps up my neck. There's nothing like literally flinging yourself at a guy to get his attention.

"Uh, sorry." I try to take a step back, but he holds on to me a beat longer.

"No worries," he says before releasing me.

I move a few feet away and try to regain some semblance of composure. I sneak a look at him out of the corner of my eye. He's looking at me with laughter in his eyes, but also maybe something else. I can't help but smile in return. I mean, it was kind of funny.

The others have stopped slightly ahead of us and are looking up. On top of the rock formation directly in front of us is a large cat. Not the domesticated kind, but a bobcat or lynx or whatever is native to these woods, and she doesn't look happy. I take a step back, and Leo puts a steadying hand on my elbow.

The cat's tail is short, and her ears have a pointed tuft of black hair at the tip. After my initial scare, I'm thinking that we aren't in any real danger, as there are six of us. But the cat is fairly big—about the size of a very large dog—and she's a wild animal with what I presume are very sharp claws and teeth. She's growling low in her throat and her ears are twitching. She could easily leap down on top of one of us.

Lorraine steps forward toward the cat. "She was coming down to the stream to drink. Her litter of cubs is hidden nearby, and we've startled her."

How does Lorraine know this? And how could we have startled her, with all the noise we were making splashing in the stream and moving along the path? I wonder, yet I'm too taken with what is going on between Lorraine and the cat to ask. They seem to have locked eyes. Lorraine holds out her hand toward the cat in a gesture of friendship. A breeze picks up and lifts Lorraine's hair out behind her in a golden curtain. She looks like a warrior goddess standing there in front of the stone wall.

The lynx curls back her lip to reveal a row of gleaming, sharp teeth, and the spotted fur along her body ripples from shoulder to rump. Then she slowly backs down from the ridge until she disappears into the bushes.

Lorraine turns toward us, her golden eyes sparkling and face glowing. "It's safe for us to pass now. She won't bother us."

"Okaay," I say as I turn to Leo, standing beside me. The others are starting up the path alongside the stream, but Leo and I hold back. "What just happened here? It looked like Lorraine was communicating with the lynx."

"Yeah, it sure did." Leo looks at the spot where the bushes swallowed the cat. "I guess I'm just glad that she could, right?" He grins at me. "Maybe she's also a forest ranger."

Or something. Uneasiness skitters across my skin.

When we finally reach the top of Greystone Mountain, my legs are rubbery from the exertion of the climb. I immediately go to sit down on one of the huge rectangular stones that lie tumbled across the flattish summit and continue down the side of the hill.

Renee comes to stand next to me and bends over at the waist. "That was a lot more difficult than I thought it would be."

She dangles her head and arms toward the leaf-strewn ground, stretching out her back and legs. "At least on the way back we'll be going downhill."

I'm thinking that just means different muscles will be sore in addition to the ones that are already overtaxed.

"What are all these stones?" Leo asks Zeke and Lorraine. He and Eric arrived at the top a few minutes ahead of us. The girls straggled a bit at the end. It's not like it was a contest—no sense in overdoing it or anything. Anyway, I'm sure the guys liked getting to the top before us, and I'm fine with that.

"These are what Greystone Mountain is named for," Zeke says. "The rocks used to be arranged in a type of henge or stone circle—similar to Stonehenge in England. The ancient Native people of the area built it to track the movements of celestial bodies in the sky, among other things."

That's cool. I wouldn't have expected that right here in southern Indiana.

"The stones were also aligned on the ley lines, or energy grid, of Earth. So are the mounds at our dig site. The stones were put in place by people who lived here prior to the settlement at the Angel Mounds site," Zeke adds.

"You're kidding, right?" Leo makes a sweeping motion with his arm to encompass the entire summit. "I mean, there must be dozens of stones here."

He's right. The stones are strewn all around us, lying flat on the ground or leaning on top of each other like giant gray Legos abandoned by a child.

"I guess they do look fairly rectangular," Leo goes on. "How did they carve them, and how the hell did they get them up here? They're massive. We're talking about people who used stone tools."

He has a point, but I don't see why it couldn't have been a henge. We don't know how the pyramids were built—or the actual Stonehenge, for that matter—so why not here too?

"Those Native cultures are only the ones that have been discovered in this area . . . so far. The people who built this were a more ancient culture than the mound builders who understood complex technologies that could move very large objects great distances and carve stone easily and with great precision. All Native cultures were more advanced spiritually and technologically than is currently believed. There's a reason we are all here at the Angel Mounds site." Zeke leans against a tree with one knee bent and his foot resting on the trunk.

What reason? I can't help but wonder.

"What kind of technology do you mean?" Renee asks as she takes off her hat to fan herself.

Lorraine walks over to where Zeke is standing. "It's time."

He nods.

"These people learned how to use their thoughts, their consciousness, to affect the world around them. By creating an antigravity field around the stones, they could lift and move them easily," Lorraine says.

Zeke has moved off to the side and is standing facing one of the larger stones that's propped up at an angle against another one lying on the ground.

Did she really mean there were people here who could lift stones with their thoughts? "What are you talking about?" I ask.

"Watch," Lorraine says.

At first nothing happens. Then energy pulses from Zeke like waves of sound reverberating against my body. But there isn't any sound. Just the physical feeling of the bass, without the music accompanying it. The air all around me snaps and crackles and vibrates in sync with the sound waves. My skin tingles.

He extends his hand toward the leaning stone and moves his arm slowly through the air. Almost imperceptibly at first, the stone starts to move, following the motion of Zeke's arm, until it's standing upright. Bright white light shoots from Zeke's fingertips. He raises his arm upward. The stone lifts off the ground and rises to hover several feet in the air.

Zeke is levitating the stone.

I realize my mouth is hanging open in amazement, and I quickly close it. I look over at the others, and the expressions on their faces are as dumbfounded as I feel. Is this really happening? Could Zeke and Lorraine have what I've been longing for? A connection to something beyond what I experience with my five senses? I know only that something has been missing from my life, but I haven't been able to figure out what it is. A flame of hope ignites inside me.

Now the white light is a web of interconnected rays, linking all of us so we're joined together, making us somehow part of what Zeke is doing and part of the energy field he's creating. I have an incredible feeling of unity with the others. It's as if I don't know where I end and they begin.

Zeke lowers his arm and comes to stand next to Lorraine. The stone remains hovering in the air behind him. "It's time to begin," he says. "You have important work to do and much to learn."

We all just stare at them, too stunned to know what to say or think. Finally, I say, "Who are you? And want exactly do you want us to do?"

5

"WE'RE HERE TO help you. You are here to help Gaia, our beautiful planet Earth, and to stop humanity from destroying her and all of the beings who call her home."

Silence hangs in the air for several minutes.

"How did you do that?" Leo demands. "How did you move the rock?"

"I used my thought energy and connected to the Universal Energy Field. Thoughts are the most powerful thing in the universe. We will show you how you can harness your own thoughts as well."

Eric stiffens and exchanges a look with Renee. He's been working on accessing the Unified Field with Renee's dad, who's a visiting physicist at the university.

"How did you learn how to . . . harness your thoughts?" I ask.

I still can't believe this is happening. The flame of hope burns inside me, but I'm also afraid. Who are Zeke and Lorraine? Can they be trusted? I want to trust them, but I barely know them. What they're showing us, the abilities they have—it's life changing. All this would seem ridiculous if it weren't for the massive block of stone that's still hovering in the air behind Zeke. And what happened earlier with Lorraine and the lynx. And the other weird things I've felt while around them.

"And would you mind lowering the stone?" I continue. "It's making me uncomfortable, hanging in the air like that."

"Sure." Zeke smiles. He sits down next to me and glances over his shoulder. The massive stone lowers slowly to the ground and gently leans back into place.

"To answer your other question, we spent many years studying with indigenous cultures and with teachers of various esoteric traditions," Lorraine says.

"Really?" Leo puts in. "I'm sure you can imagine that this is a little—no, make that a *lot*—hard to believe. That primitive cultures know how to do this, but the rest of the world doesn't?"

"Well, they're hardly primitive in the sense of their metaphysical knowledge, just in terms of modern technological advancements, which they don't need in light of their abilities," Lorraine says. "And some people in powerful positions do have this knowledge and choose not to share it out of greed and the desire for power and control." She cocks her head to one side as if welcoming a contradictory response from Leo. "Of course, it's outside of your realm of experience—but not, I think, outside the realm of your imagination? You can see with your own eyes that this is true."

"Yeah, I guess so."

Zeke looks over at Eric. "Some of you already have experience accessing the Unified Field with your thoughts."

How could he know that? Did he read our thoughts, like it seemed he did when I first saw him in the clearing, or does he somehow know more about us than he should?

"Did you just read my thoughts?" Eric asks.

"We have the ability to read your thought vibrations. You have the ability to shield your thoughts if you don't wish to share them. I was aware that you wanted to ask the question, so I answered it," Zeke says. "I meant no disrespect to you."

"It's OK," Eric tells him. "Just a little weird, you know?"

"Many people in governments across the planet do know about thought energy and other technologies and wish to keep that knowledge a secret," Zeke continues. "The United States has been using remote viewing for years to spy on other countries' military installations. They're concerned about what would happen if the general population knew how to harness thought energy. There are people in government who wish to keep power to themselves and have little regard for the Earth and her inhabitants."

This sounds ominous. Could our government be manipulating us and hiding things? Unfortunately, it's not hard to believe.

"If we accept what you're telling us is true," I say, "what exactly are you here to help us do? We're just a few teenagers. How can we help the save the Earth?"

Lorraine looks at me. "All beings, including all of you, are vastly more powerful than you realize," she says. "Zeke and I are here to teach you. When it's time, you will be ready, and you'll know what to do. Earth is in a crisis due to greed and destruction brought on by fear and power mongering. There are many who are destroying the planet and exploiting the population of Earth for their own personal gain. Fortunately, there are also many on Earth who focus on love and spiritual growth. You four are on the side of love. For now, just know that you are learning. More will come."

Not helpful.

I look at Leo. It seems odd that he's being included as he seems so resistant to what they're showing us. I'm happy that he's here for my own reasons but have to question Zeke and Lorraine's judgement. Maybe they know something I don't.

"It will be most enlightening if you can see for yourselves what's in store for Earth if nothing changes the current path of humanity," Lorraine says. "I'll lead you in a guided meditation, and Zeke will share the images with you." She moves to the stone closest to her and sits down.

Zeke, on the slab next to mine, gives me a reassuring look.

"Are all of you comfortable with that?" Lorraine softens her tone. "There's nothing to fear."

"Yes," I answer, not sure if the butterflies in my stomach indicate excitement or apprehension or a little of both. What are we getting ourselves into?

"Just sit comfortably, close your eyes, and rest your hands in your lap. You'll be seeing with your inner eye, your inner knowing." Lorraine speaks rhythmically, her voice becoming melodious. The sound flows over me in a warm, comforting wave.

"Focus on your breathing. Breathe in . . . breathe out. Breathe in . . . breathe out."

I breathe in slowly for a count of four and release the breath for a count of four. Lorraine continues guiding us in our breathing for several minutes, and my body relaxes as my thoughts settle and move inward.

"Now we will show you one of the possibilities for the future of Earth. This is just a possibility, not a definite future. It can be changed. It's what we're here to do."

I'm aware of the presence of Zeke entering my mind, asking my permission to share his thoughts with me. It's not an unpleasant sensation; it doesn't feel like an intrusion. I open my mind to him, and images begin to flicker in my mind's eye.

Before me is a curtain of red velvet. I push the curtain aside to find a large window. Through the window, I see a vast desert, but not of sand. Dry earth, cracked and parched. Dead vegetation. Desiccated trees and brittle bushes. No animal life at all. Desolate and barren.

The next image is of water. A bird's-eye view. The ocean, covered with a gray, oily film. Bits of trash and plastic floating past. An island of garbage that must be as large as Hawaii, roiling on the surface, growing ever larger.

The scene moves toward the shore, and I see buildings in the water. Skyscrapers sticking up out of the waves. Cities flooded. Then the view pans further inland, and the air shimmers with heat and humidity. Vegetation grows wild, overtaking buildings and roads. There are no people in the images, but I know they are there, and an overpowering feeling of fear and anguish emanates from them. And from Earth herself.

Next I see the remains of a forest ravaged by fire. The trees stand like burned matchsticks, black against a hazy, gray sky. An enormous, gaping hole filled with rubble.

Everywhere Earth is out of balance. In extreme drought, or excess growth, or flooding. There's a feeling of aloneness, separateness. It's physically and emotionally devastating. Tears well up in my eyes. I'm overcome with emotion at the loss and destruction, the abandonment and desolation. I let the red curtain fall. It's too much to take in.

Lorraine's soothing voice penetrates my thoughts. "Continue breathing. Breathe in . . . breathe out. Breathe in . . . breathe out."

I'm comforted by her words, and the horrifying images recede.

"When you're ready, you can open your eyes," she says.

I take one final breath and open my eyes, blinking owlishly at the others. Did they see what I saw? Did they feel what I felt? Everyone looks a little unfocused.

I turn to Eric and whisper, "Did you see it? The Earth destroyed?"

"Yeah," he says quietly. He swallows and nods. "I did."

"I saw it too." Renee leans forward and puts her face in her hands. Her voice is muffled through her fingers. "It's too awful to think about that happening."

I feel the same way, but I'm not yet able to put my thoughts into words. My emotions are still raw from the experience.

"Thank you, Zeke, for sharing those images with all of us," Lorraine says after a few moments. Zeke only nods, but I can feel his reassuring thoughts still present in my mind.

"Now you know," she continues softly, but her eyes are fierce, "about the terrible future that awaits Earth and humanity if we continue on our current path." She pauses, placing her hands on the stone on either side of her legs and leaning forward for emphasis. "It can be changed. Are you ready to do your part? Will you allow us to teach you so that you know your own power?"

I want to do whatever I can to stop the destruction I witnessed in the vision. Maybe this is what I've been waiting for: a mission and a purpose, connecting with the collective consciousness. I feel a little like I'm stepping off a cliff into the unknown, but if I don't move forward, I know I'll regret it.

I take a deep, calming breath. "Yes, I'm ready."

"How do you know about what will happen in the future?" Leo's posture is rigid, his voice cutting. "There's no reason to believe any of it's true."

"You're right in part. There's no way to definitively know the future. Thousands of possibilities exist with different probabilities. However, what Zeke showed you will very likely happen if we continue to disregard the well-being of Earth. She can only accommodate so much abuse before her equilibrium is tilted irrevocably. Already floods, hurricanes, fires, volcanoes, and tsunamis are increasing in frequency and strength." I note that she only answers part of Leo's question. How are they able to predict the future at all, even if it is just one of many possibilities?

Renee says what all of us are probably thinking, at least a little. "I want to help, but I'm afraid. This is all so much to take in." Her French accent is very strong, so she must be feeling really agitated.

"Yeah, I agree." Eric puts his arm behind her back, bracing her. "Can you give us some time to move slowly on this? I mean . . . we *just* found out that you two are both some kind of shaman, and now you want us to save the world?" His weak attempt at a joke falls flat.

"This is a lot to take in. And honestly, I'm not sure I'm buying any of this." Leo looks both bewildered and defiant. He's probably wondering what the hell he got himself into, hanging out with the Hortons, but why does he have to be so resistant?

"Of course. You're right," Lorraine says. "This is enough for now. There's much to learn. You don't have to decide yet. Just know this is the path you each chose. You intended for this to be your life's work."

"What are you talking about?" Eric asks.

"All will become clear in time. Be patient," Lorraine says cryptically.

So much for not putting the pressure on or making us choose. I hope I'm ready.

"I'm going to head back on my own. I'll wait for you all down by the car." Leo jumps up and takes off down the trail before anyone replies. He's practically running to get away.

No one tries to stop him.

The rest of us hang around the clearing to gather ourselves a little before the return hike, but nobody says much. It's hard to have small talk after discussing the devastation of Earth. Plus,

36

Zeke and Lorraine are there, so the rest of us can't really talk much in front of them.

Suddenly Renee grabs Eric's hand and pulls him several yards away. She's wild eyed and frantic. I can't hear what they're saying, but Eric has his hands on her shoulders and his face is only inches from hers. Renee's reaction to the visions appears to be fear. I'm afraid too. Believing Zeke and Lorraine can affect the world around them with only their thoughts—and that they'll show me how to do it—alters everything I thought previously about how the world works. It's like I just stepped into a different dimension.

Eric and Renee lead the way down the mountain, and I follow. Zeke and Lorraine are directly behind me. They're talking quietly, but I can hear what they're saying. I think they want me to hear them. Wouldn't they communicate telepathically with each other if they didn't want me to?

"They're not ready," Lorraine says. "It's too soon."

"It had to be now," Zeke answers. "You know that. It will take time, but they'll begin to see and understand. As we show them more and their abilities strengthen, they'll come around."

"I wasn't expecting their reactions to be this strong. Maybe we revealed too much too soon."

"Maybe. But Marcie and Eric are ready to begin. Perhaps they can help by leading the way." Is this what they wanted me to hear? Do they want me to help with Renee and Leo?

"Yes, let's hope so," Lorraine says.

A wave of anxiety surges through me. I don't know if I can do this. Why does this have to be my responsibility anyway? How can I lead someone else when I don't even really understand what's happening to me or what's expected of us? Aren't there other people on Earth who'd be thrilled to sign up to save the world? I suddenly realize I've already accepted Zeke and Lorraine's advanced abilities, and I understand that they're here to help us. I just don't know if I can or want to take the lead.

Leo is leaning against the car when we reach the parking area, his posture stiff and his arms crossed over his chest.

"Why did you leave like that?" I ask him, even though I think I know why.

"I just had to get away from there. From them." He looks under lowered lids to where Zeke and Lorraine are coming down the path behind me.

"But why?" I can understand not being fully convinced or not wanting to be involved, but I don't understand his anger and antagonism toward them. "They're here to help us. Don't you see?"

"No, I don't," he says through gritted teeth. "I want no part of this, whatever it is. Just leave me out of it." He opens the door of the SUV and climbs into the far back seat, leaving me feeling slightly ill and off balance.

Maybe I'm not being very understanding, but I want to share this experience with him. I climb in and fight to compose myself. We all ride in silence back to the dig site.

ALL THROUGH DINNER I watch Lorraine and Zeke to see if something about them would suddenly make them seem different, now that I know what they are capable of. But they look just the same as they have all week, like perfectly normal human beings.

Questions swirl in a random jumble through my mind and I can't make sense of any of it. Why me, why us? What do Lorraine and Zeke want us to do exactly? What if I can't do it—or I don't want to? Can I decide not to?

Renee's question brings me back to the moment.

"Do you think the visions were real?" She's folding and unfolding her napkin into geometric shapes.

The four of us stayed at the table after we finished eating in an unspoken agreement to talk over what happened on the mountain. Even Leo seems to want to sort out what we experienced.

"I don't know what to think, really. I mean, it's all so crazy, but we're sitting here talking about it, so I guess it really happened," Eric says. "It's not like I have all the answers, though."

"But do you think it's *true*?" Leo asks. "What they said about what could happen to the Earth?" The frank openness of his question after his angry behavior early in the afternoon compels me to say what I really think.

"Yeah, it could be true. I know for sure that we're destroying Earth."

Leo shakes his head. "It feels like a bunch of bullshit to me. There's no way we're capable of destroying the Earth." He looks at me as if he's challenging me to contradict him. "Maybe it was some sort of group hypnosis, I don't know . . . but shamans with thought control powers? No way is that true."

I reply slowly, trying to put how I'm feeling into words. Talking with the others has helped me to clarify my thoughts. "I can see why you would think that. They're making pretty incredible claims, but even if I don't understand what's going on, I'm open to it. I've always thought there was more to the world than what we normally perceive. I've even had some personal experience with that. And I do really think Lorraine and Zeke can use thought energy to affect the world around them. We saw the stone levitate. It's what they want *us* to do that I'm not sure about."

"But what if their intentions aren't what they say?" Renee's eyes fill with concern. "What if they really mean to cause us harm?"

This had also occurred to me when I first encountered Zeke and Lorraine. A brief flutter of unease churns my stomach, but I force myself to dismiss the idea.

"They don't want to harm us. They want to save the planet."

"You can't really know that for certain," Renee says.

But I can hope.

6

"YOUR DAD'S COMING down tomorrow afternoon with your brother," my mom says as she sits down next to me and snags a piece of banana out of my bowl of cereal. I'm sitting at the table in the dining room of the girls' dorm. The other girls move around us, getting their own breakfasts. Renee left early to eat with Eric. Lainey and Nora were still getting dressed when I came down.

"He is?" I'm surprised to hear this.

Usually my mom goes *home* on the weekends, if at all, and my dad doesn't often come to the dig site, especially as he has to bring Drew and there isn't much for a ten-year-old to do. It's unusual that the roles would be reversed, that he's coming here instead. She reaches for another banana slice, and I block her with my shoulder.

"Hey, get your own banana. There's a bunch on the counter by the sink."

"But I don't want a whole banana, just a few slices." She puts on a fake sad face but stops stealing my bananas. "Anyway, your dad and Mr. Clement have contacted farmers in the area and are holding a meeting on Saturday at Nana and Pop's farm about United Energy's plans to expand fracking in the area."

Mr. Clement is a family friend. He's also an environmental attorney.

"Wow, that was fast. We only just heard about the fracking a couple of days ago." I eat several spoonsful of cereal as my mom continues talking.

"Yes, well, Mr. Clement thinks we need to act quickly to build up public awareness of the dangers of fracking before United Energy comes around waving big wads of money to get the mineral rights on the farmland. He's asked a farmer from Pennsylvania to come and talk about what happened to his land and water after they fracked the wells on his property."

"Can I come to the meeting?"

"We're counting on students from the dig attending." She pushes herself into a standing position. "There's power in numbers, and that's the biggest thing we have on our side. That and the facts about the dangers of fracking. You know United Energy is going to push hard to get this through. It represents a lot of money for them."

I'm reminded of what Lorraine said about power and greed destroying the Earth. Maybe this is how I can help.

"OK, I'll see who else wants to come." I get up from the table and rinse my bowl in the sink before putting it in the dishwasher.

"That's great, honey. I knew I could count on you." She puts her hand on the side of my face, and for a moment I think she's going to kiss my forehead—but seeing the look on my face, she just gives my cheek a little pat before leaving. "See you at the site," she tells me.

TODAY I'M PAIRED with Leo and Lainey on hoeing duty. We're just about finished with all of the hoeing, and hopefully we'll begin actual excavating on Friday. It's another hot, sunny day. I adjust my bandana to protect the back of my neck from the sun. So far the sweat-proof sunscreen I brought has been living up to its name, which is a good thing, as far as I can say. My fair skin will burn in a matter of minutes without it. Leo's olive skin doesn't burn, though. He's just turning a lovely shade of caramel, which I find that much more attractive.

We haven't talked much since yesterday in the parking lot after the hike, but I've been surreptitiously sneaking looks at him all morning. On our hike up Greystone Mountain, I'd thought maybe there was something developing between us. But either I imagined it—or it all got washed away when he lashed out at me because of how I reacted to what Lorraine and Zeke said and showed us. I'm still strongly attracted to him in spite of his resistance to them. I can't seem to help it. But I don't know if he feels the same about me.

Our eyes meet as I'm studying him from under my lashes, and I quickly look away. I sigh, put my gloves back on, and pick up my hoe. A shadow falls across the area where I'm working, and a pair of boots comes into view in my peripheral vision. I feel a hand on my shoulder and look up to see Leo silhouetted against the sky.

"Hey," he says. I straighten and move so that his head blocks the sun behind him.

"Hey," I reply. I can't help but notice the deep brown of his eyes is almost exactly the same color as his hair. His hair is a mess, but I want to reach out and touch it.

"I wanted to apologize for yesterday. I shouldn't have gotten mad at you." He's wringing his hands. He startles me by reaching for my hand. I'm surprised, so I instinctively start to pull my hand away, but he holds on tightly and pulls me toward him. "I'm sorry. I know you're excited about Lorraine and Zeke and what they told us. I'm just not there. I don't know whether I'll ever get there."

"It's OK," I say. "I should apologize too. I wasn't being very nice about how you were feeling. I think I understand where you're coming from, though." I try to sound offhand, but my heart has started pounding because I'm not sure what it means that he's holding my hand.

"Good. I hope you do understand, because I want us to be friends." He's staring at me with those beautiful brown eyes. What does he mean, *friends*?

"Still friends," I reply.

Scott chooses that moment to walk past us.

He cocks an eyebrow and looks back and forth between us. "What have we here?"

"None of your business." Leo drops my hand, but he winks at me and squeezes my fingers before he lets them go.

LATER ON LAINEY, Leo, and I are taking a water break, sitting on the compacted clay soil, when I remember the conversation I had with my mom earlier that morning.

"My dad and my little brother are coming down on Saturday." I try to scrape off some of the clay that's caked on the soles of my boots with the edge of my hoe, but the effort is futile. More clay will just cover them when I stand up. My legs are streaked with tan clay up to my knees. "My dad is organizing a meeting of local farmers so they can talk about United Energy's fracking plans for the area. They're holding the meeting on my grandparents' farm."

"Really?" Leo's interest perks up. "Is United Energy going to be there too? I'd like to go to that."

"I don't think you get it. We're opposed to fracking. United Energy won't be there."

Leo shakes his head. "*You* guys don't get it. Fracking is good for America. Natural gas is the future."

"Scott told me stories of farmers in Kansas who've allowed fracking on their land. There are terrible side effects. Undrinkable well water and dying livestock. It is *not* good for America," Lainey says. "Where do you get your information?"

He takes a drink from his water bottle. "My dad works for the Department of Energy. He gets his information from the gas and oil companies—and they say it's safe."

"Puh!" The indignant sound escapes from my mouth. "Of course that's what they say! Deny, deny, deny. Until it's too late. Isn't that what the tobacco companies did? Denied that smoking causes cancer?"

"The fracking chemicals they use are totally unregulated. They're basically pumping poison into our aquifers," Lainey says.

"OK, OK." Leo holds up his hands in surrender and smiles. "I can see that I'm outnumbered here. But I'd still like to come to the meeting. That is, if I'm allowed." His teeth gleam against his tan as he smiles at me.

His capitulation takes the heat out of my argument, which might have been his intention. But I like Leo in spite of our disagreeing on the so-called benefits of fracking. I'm just not sure at this point if it's a deal breaker for me. If I'm being honest with myself, what I'm really hoping is that I can change his opinion over time.

"Sure, you can come." I stand up, brush the dirt off my shorts, and pull my gloves back on. "Back to work, I guess."

"I am so ready to start excavating," Leo says. "This hoeing feels too much like manual labor." He dumps another clump of dirt into his bucket. "I think this is full enough to be screened." He carries it over to where Eric, Renee, and Scott are screening.

We haven't seen much of Lorraine and Zeke today. They got us started on the hoeing and screening and went off to do some surveying work. I wondered how our interactions would be with them after the events of yesterday afternoon, but they're acting completely normal. As if nothing has changed. It's the rest of us who are acting differently. I certainly feel changed.

Just as Leo leaves to "dump his load," as we've been affectionately referring to the transfer of dirt from the site to the screens, Lorraine comes over to see how we're doing. "This looks great!" she says. "I think tomorrow we can begin excavating."

"That's good news," Lainey replies as she moves several yards away to start hoeing again.

Lorraine turns to me. "I heard your parents are having a meeting with local farmers on Saturday about fracking in the area." I nod in agreement.

"Zeke and I would like to come, if that's all right."

"That depends on if you're for or against fracking." I'm joking, of course. I'd love for them to come and I'm fairly certain they're against it, given what they showed us in the visions.

"Obviously we're opposed!"

"Yes, we'd love for you to come. We're trying to see if more people from the dig want to come too." I hesitate for a moment and look around to see if anyone is within earshot, but the other students are focused on their own tasks. I lower my voice anyway.

"Does this meeting have anything to do with how we can help the Earth? Are we supposed to do something about fracking in this area?" It feels a little strange to be talking about our mission, such as it is, in the middle of the dig site with everyone else around.

Normal life continues while something extraordinary is happening.

"Yes, part of what you're to do is raise awareness of how fracking and other destructive practices like burning fossil fuels are causing great harm to Earth."

"What are we supposed to do, exactly?"

"More will be revealed to you in time. You must be patient as you learn and as the process unfolds. You'll be guided and will know what to do when the time comes." Her vagueness is irritating. I like to know exactly how things are going to go.

Lorraine puts her hand on my shoulder and a calming energy emanates from her. "I know this is frustrating for you. We're asking you to place a great deal of trust in us, and I understand that it's hard not knowing what to expect or how you can help. But everything is happening just the way it's supposed to, and you will be ready to do your part. That's all you need to know for now."

I take a deep breath and release the tension in my shoulders as I exhale. "OK. I'm OK with that."

"You won't have to wait long. Saturday night we'd like to go to the top of Emerald Mound and have another meeting. Will you tell the others?"

"Tell the others what?" Leo says as he joins us, swinging his now empty bucket.

"That we'll be having another meeting on Emerald Mound on Saturday night," I say warily.

As much as I want Leo to be part of what's going on with Zeke and Lorraine, his resistance makes me wonder if maybe he shouldn't be included.

"Oh." His smile fades and his face shutters.

"I really hope you'll come." Why do I want him there so badly? Is it because I like him and I want to share this with him? He's so obviously resistant. Or is it that I want to try to convert him to my point of view? And why are Zeke and Lorraine including him as he's not at all on board? Wouldn't it be better to include someone like Scott since he's already a climate change advocate? But then, Renee doesn't completely accept Zeke and Lorraine even though she's opposed to fracking. Maybe the point is trying to reach people and open their minds to what's happening and what's possible. All I know is that I very much want him to be part of it.

"Yeah, maybe." He scuffs the dirt with the toe of his boot.

Lorraine steps in. "I'm going to talk to Dr. Horton and Dr. Fraser about having a group demonstration after lunch on excavating techniques as well as how to measure and catalogue features of your site and any artifacts you find."

"Cool. Now we're talking." The shuttered look on his face vanishes, and Leo drops his bucket on the ground and raises his arms over his head. "This is why I came on the field study: to find artifacts."

"Good. You and Marcie finish up here. I'm going to find Dr. Horton. When you're done, will you let the screening team know it's time to break for lunch? I'll see you all later." She turns quickly and her braid swings around behind her as she walks away.

"What do you guys think about Lorraine and Zeke?" Lainey asks as she helps us scrape up the remaining loose dirt and deposit it into our buckets.

"What do you mean?" I reply, alarmed.

"I don't know. They just seem a little different somehow. Kind of aloof, and they keep to themselves, but they're really intense, you know?" She's bent over her bucket and looks back over her shoulder at me.

I glance briefly at Leo before answering. "I guess so, but they're no different from any of the other graduate students

I've met over the years. They all tend to take themselves pretty seriously." Why do I feel the need to protect Zeke and Lorraine? They *are* different. There's no denying it. I sensed it immediately upon meeting them so it's no surprise that Lainey does too. I guess I don't want what I see as extraordinary interpreted as being weird.

"Yeah, that's probably what it is." She straightens and dusts her hands on her shorts.

"Ladies, I think our work here is done." Leo puts his hands on his hips. "I'll take the hoes back to the trailer and hope that I never have to see them again. Let's get some lunch."

7

After lunch everyone gathers around Dr. Fraser for a demonstration on excavating our individual sites. Archaeology is a destructive science. When we excavate a site, we are literally destroying it, so it's important to take lots of notes and measurements of what we find.

He's explaining how to establish a data point elevation for our section so we can indicate how far down the artifacts we find are from the surface. It's important stuff, but I find my mind wandering. Grasshoppers are buzzing in the grass surrounding us, and the monotonous sound, combined with the heat of the day, is lulling me to sleep.

I entertain myself by observing Zeke and Lorraine. Lorraine sits cross-legged on the ground toward the front of the group, and Zeke is standing in the back with the taller students. They're dressed like everyone else in the usual shorts, T-shirt, boots, and hat. I keep wondering who they are, really. Where did they come from?

I'm jarred out of my thoughts by the sunlight glinting off Dr. Fraser's glasses. Sweat runs in rivulets down his face, and he removes his hat and glasses to mop his face with his bandana. His thinning red hair is plastered to his head. Scott is shifting from foot to foot next to me.

"When you're excavating at your location, you want to use your trowel to gently scrape off layers of dirt." Dr. Fraser picks up his trowel and scrapes a small area to demonstrate. "If you think you've found something, just call your team leader over to take a look." He sits back on his heels. "That's it then. You're all ready to get started. For the rest of the afternoon, we'll set up your sections and data points. Monday we'll start excavating."

Everyone is pleased with this and quickly disperses to their sections of the site. I tap Scott on the shoulder as he's turning to go.

"I don't know if anyone told you, but we're having a meeting at my grandparents' farm on Saturday about fracking. A family friend who's an environmental attorney is coming, and he's bringing someone from Pennsylvania to talk about what fracking did to his land and water. It'd be great if you'd come, too, and maybe share a little of your experience."

"I'd love to come. Those big energy companies are selling a pack of lies and writing hefty checks. Count me in," he says.

"Thanks. We'll leave about 9:30am."

THAT NIGHT AFTER dinner, instead of hanging around the bonfire with the rest of the group, Eric and Renee and Leo and I decide to take a walk down to the Ohio River. When we enter the shelter of the woods around the dorms Leo reaches for my hand. I'm startled in a good way and let out an involuntary gasp. I peek at him out of the corner of my eye, wondering if he noticed. His roughened palm is hard and cool. Hopefully mine isn't sticky and hot.

The long grass of the field surrounding the mounds gives off the spicy smell of clover and wild onions in the warm, humid air. The shadowy hulk of Angel Mound rises up to our right, and the smaller Emerald Mound sits on the opposite end of the field closer to the river. Stars pinprick the inky blackness of the night sky above; there are far more of them visible here than back home, where there's always light pollution.

"I've been thinking about what Zeke said—about everything being connected and about using the Field to levitate the stone," Eric says. "Do you think it's the same thing as what we're trying to do in the lab with your dad, Renee?" Eric's told me about working with Renee's dad, Dr. Auberge, in his physics lab, doing experiments to access the Universal Energy Field. Dr. Auberge believes there's a current of thought energy connecting everything in the universe.

"Probably. That would make sense," Renee replies without much enthusiasm.

"It's like another confirmation of how everything is inter-related and that we are on the right track with our research." He swings their clasped hands as they walk down the path. "I mean, I'm still trying to process what happened on Greystone Mountain, but this is *real*, not just an experiment in the lab."

Beside me, Leo is silent, but the tension radiating off him is palpable.

"I know. That's the problem," Renee says. We've reached the stand of trees that line the shore of the river. It's very dark in the woods, so we're silent as we navigate the trail. The path opens to a small bluff overlooking the water. There's a bench off to the left of the path. Eric and Renee and I sit down, and Leo sits on the ground next to me.

Eric turns to face Renee. "Is something wrong?"

"I don't know." She wraps her arms around herself. "It's just that I'm feeling really anxious about what's happening."

"I can understand that," I say. "I'm a little apprehensive about it, too, but also excited. Imagine if everyone could control their thoughts like Zeke and Lorraine."

"I thought that you of all people would be more on board with it," Eric says to Renee. "We've been working with your dad on similar stuff for a long time now."

"You mean *you've* been working with him. I'm participating in the experiments, but I'm not having the same experiences as you. I'm not connecting with the Field." Now her voice has an edge to it.

"I didn't know that bothered you—and you *are* connecting."

I don't say anything because this seems to be an issue between the two of them. Leo is leaning against my legs now but has remained silent.

"You're right. I know I connect on some level. Just not to the extent that you do," Renee says. "It's just that those images we saw were awful. How do we know Zeke and Lorraine are here to help us? What if it they want to do us harm?" Her words rush out. She takes a deep breath and exhales audibly. "I really want to believe them. I'm just afraid."

I tentatively put my hand on Leo's shoulder, and he reaches up to entwine our fingers. He seems to have relaxed somewhat, but now my heart is pounding.

"I'm a little afraid too," I say. "And I'm not sure what this all means for us because we don't know what exactly they want us to do, but I'm also excited. We can learn so much from them."

The sound of the river flowing past and lapping at the shore reaches us from below. Something splashes in the water, and the musty smell of damp and mud permeates the air. We're absorbed in our own thoughts for several minutes. There's so much running through my head that I'd like to talk about with Leo, but I'm not sure if I should. At least he's still here.

"Do you mind if we don't talk about it anymore?" Renee says. "I think I've had enough of shamans and energy fields to last me for a while."

"OK," Eric says.

I guess he and I will have to talk to each other . . . and to Zeke and Lorraine. Surely they can provide answers instead of provoking more questions.

Leo and I hold hands on the way back to the dorms. When we reach the darkest part of the woods, he stops and turns toward me. His outline is indistinct against the darkness of the trees, but we are close enough that I can see his face in the shadows.

"A bunch of us are going canoeing on the river tomorrow afternoon." He looks down for a moment. "I was, uh, wondering if you'd like to come with us . . . with me."

Is he asking me on a date? "Yeah, I would. Sounds like fun," I tell him. I'm glad now for the shadows partially hiding the expression on my face, which is sure to reveal precisely how excited I am about going.

"Great." Leo's mouth quirks up at the corners, and he rakes a hand through his hair, making it messier than it already was. "I was afraid you might say no since I'm not totally on board with Zeke and Lorraine and the whole fracking thing."

"Nah, that's OK. You're wrong about fracking, though." I give him a soft jab in the stomach.

"We can just agree to disagree—for now," he says. "Let's meet in the shelter area around three o'clock. Wear your bathing suit. You're bound to get wet."

We walk back to the dorms in companionable silence.

8

SINCE SOME OF the students go home for the weekend, we quit work at two thirty on Fridays. I gather up all my gear and head back to my room to change into my bathing suit for my "date" with Leo. I'm a little nervous, but also excited about the whole canoeing adventure. That's what I decide to call it: an adventure. I'm not sure if it's an actual date, but it'll be fun, whatever it is. I put on a pair of khaki shorts and a red scoop-neck T-shirt over my suit. I can always take them off. I rifle through my drawer for my tote bag and stuff a towel and sunscreen into it.

Leo is already sitting on the picnic table bench when I get to the shelter. He stands up and reaches for my hand. It's nice that he's so forthright about showing how he feels, but I'm still not entirely used to his touch and how it makes my nerves jump and my skin tingle. He does look awfully cute in his blue and white block-printed swim trunks, flip-flops, and faded blue T-shirt, though.

"Are you ready to get wet?" He tugs on my hand.

"Are you planning on tipping the canoe or something?" The nervousness creeps into my voice, but he's looking at me with such frank interest that my excitement is getting the upper hand.

"Or something," he says archly. "Have you ever been canoeing before?"

"Sure, but I try not to tip over the canoe."

"Well, I plan to be in the back of the canoe, steering, which puts you in the front, right in the line of possible splashing."

"I see. Then I'll have to think of some way to defend myself. I'll have a paddle, too, you know." I give him a sly look.

"I guess we're both forewarned then." He looks over toward the parking area. "We'd better head over. The others are gathering by the cars."

We load into two cars and drive a short distance to a canoe rental area on the bank of the river. The water flows past the shore, a murky green-brown color. The weather is nice today, and several trucks and SUVs back down the boat ramp, slowly edging boats into the water. Many more are parked in the lot with empty boat trailers, so I imagine quite a few boats are already out on the water.

As I'm getting my life jacket from a peg on the wall of the rental shed, Lainey comes up next to me.

"You're going to share a canoe with Leo?" she asks, raising her eyebrows.

"Yes," I say slowly. I can't help the smile tugging at the corners of my mouth.

"Lucky you." Her gaze flicks to where Leo and Scott are standing by the canoes. "Now if I can only get Scott to notice me." She grins. "Have fun!"

"Thanks!"

Leo and I carry our canoe down to the shore and climb in. The rental operators give us a push, and the boat glides into the water with barely a ripple. At first we stay close to the other canoes, and Leo splashes me a few times by dipping his oar into the water and swinging it in an arc so droplets of water splatter me. It's not enough to really soak me—it's more refreshing than anything else.

After a while he stops paddling as hard, and we lag behind a bit. We come up to a small island near the shore. The trees lean out over the water, trailing vines and branches into the current. Leo steers us into the tunnel they form. We can still see the others not far ahead of us, but I'm not sure if they can easily see us.

The canoe bumps into the bank of the island, and we stop. I'm about to push us away with my oar when the boat starts rocking, and Leo says, "Wait."

I twist around to find that he's right behind me. "Turn around all the way," he says.

I'm getting a little short of breath in anticipation of what I think is coming. *Is he going to kiss me?* I lift my legs over the seat so I'm facing him. He's on his knees and a little unsteady; the boat is narrow at the end, and there isn't much room.

"I've been wanting to do this all day." He leans forward to kiss me.

I close my eyes and my lips part when his lips meet mine. He tastes salty and a little bit like coconut oil from his sunscreen. Only our lips touch at first because he's holding on to the sides of the boat with both hands, and I'm too nervous to reach out to him. The longer we kiss, the bolder I feel, so I put my hand behind his head and curl my fingers into his hair, which is what *I've* been wanting to do all day.

He reaches his arm around me and pulls me to him so our bodies are pressed together. I'm finding it a little hard to breathe, and the feel of him against me almost takes the rest of my breath away. I put my other arm around him. *We are making out in a boat in the middle of the river.*

All of a sudden, Leo's knee slips, and he lurches into me and knocks us both off balance. The boat rocks violently, and we fall over the side into the water with an enormous splash. I come up sputtering and look for Leo.

He emerges about two yards away from me and shakes the hair out of his eyes. "I can't believe that happened. I'm so sorry. So much for romance. Are you OK?"

We're both treading water and moving toward the boat, which is somehow still upright.

"I'm fine. You *did* warn me that I would get wet today." I reach for the side of the boat and tread water while holding on. Thankfully all our stuff is still in the canoe; only Leo and I were dumped out. "I didn't think you were really going to dunk me, though."

He's come up beside me. We're both hanging on to the side of the boat with our faces close together, just out of the water. He looks incredible with his dark hair plastered to his head and droplets of water clinging to his eyelashes.

"But I forgive you." I lean forward to kiss him again.

Our legs entwine under the water. Leo uses the leverage to pull me closer to him and kisses me back.

WE TRY TO climb back into the canoe from the water, but that proves to be impossible without tipping it over completely. We end up hauling ourselves onto the island using the tree roots and vines to pull ourselves up. We climb into the boat from there. I go first while Leo holds it steady, then he gets in.

At this point, the others have turned around to look for us, and it's a big joke when we paddle out of the tunnel soaking wet. I don't mind. The kiss—well, both kisses—were totally worth getting dunked.

My clothes are still damp by the time we maneuver the canoe back to the shore at the launch site. They smell fishy and musty, and I'm totally going to have to do laundry. The talk on the car ride back is all about what everyone is going to do over the weekend. Leo's beside me in the back seat.

I say quietly to him, "Are you going to Emerald Mound with us tomorrow night?"

"I don't know. I'm not really sure I want to."

I get that he's not totally on board, but I persist anyway. "After dunking me in the river, I think you owe it to me to come."

"Maybe." He hunches his shoulders forward.

"I'll come by to get you, and we can walk over together." I hope that if I make it seem like another "date" he'll decide to go. "Will you come, please?"

He sighs. "I guess I have to, since you said please." He tugs a lock of my straggly, probably smelly hair and links his fingers with mine.

I squeeze his hand as tiny explosions of happiness burst in my chest.

9

"COME ON, LEO, ride with us," I say.

Everyone is piling into cars for the short drive to the Horton farm for the fracking meeting. Even though we made up the other day, Leo hasn't been completely at ease with me since the events on the mountain. During the day on the site, he's been keeping his distance from the rest of our team as much as he can. And he's been spending the evenings with some of the other students . . . which is fine. He can hang out with whomever he wants, but I feel like I'm getting mixed messages from him. Does he like me or not? On the river I thought he was definitely into me, but sometimes when I'm around him I've felt a simmering anger emanating from him, which I don't really understand. I get that he might be freaked out by what happened on Greystone Mountain, but why would he be angry?

Leo looks from me over to Zeke's SUV, where Zeke and Lorraine are climbing in with three girls from another team.

"You don't have to go with them," I say quietly. "You don't even have to be near them. Ride with us. Three can fit in the back seat." I indicate Renee already in the back.

Eric and Scott are in the front. They're waiting for me to get in.

"Please," I add. I've revised my feelings about him being part of our group, such as it is. I think it's important he continue to be involved with whatever is happening with Zeke and Lorraine. They did include him in our Greystone Mountain experience. Also, I really want him to come with us, with me. Maybe he'll change his thinking about fracking.

"OK." His face relaxes, and I'm rewarded with a small smile. "I'd love to come with you."

The tightness in my chest eases. Before he can change his mind, I scramble into the back seat next to Renee. He squeezes in beside me.

"Let's go," I say to Eric.

I'm very conscious of Leo's thigh in contact with the length of my leg and his shoulder pressed into mine. Renee nudges me in the side with her elbow. I told her a little bit of how I'm starting to feel about Leo.

"How are you?" She leans across me and directs her question to Leo. "You've been kind of scarce since Greystone Mountain."

I cringe a little. Renee's not afraid to get right to the point, but I think it would have been better to open with a little more finesse.

Leo flushes and looks a little uncomfortable. "Yeah, I know." He purses his lips. "But it's not because of you guys. I really like all of you. It's just that I'm still working through the stuff that happened on Greystone Mountain, you know? I'm not sure I want to be part of whatever Zeke and Lorraine have in mind."

I look to see if Scott overhead this, but he and Eric have the music turned up in the front.

"I know what you mean exactly," Renee says. "I find it all very bizarre."

I don't want to alienate Leo by starting a big discussion about what I think—right when he's finally back connecting with us, with *me*—so I just say, "I think that's totally understandable, but it doesn't mean you have to keep your distance from us."

"You're right. It doesn't." He puts his hand lightly on my leg. It's not really a big deal, but somehow the gesture seems intimate, possessive. I cover his hand with mine and link my fingers through his. A secret smile tugs at the corners of my mouth.

Over twenty of the students and faculty from the dig are attending the meeting. My mom is going, of course, as well as Dr. Fraser. Zeke and Lorraine are going, and, since I convinced Leo to come, everyone on my team will be there. The other four grad students and eight of the college students make up the rest of the four carloads driving in a caravan down the highway.

The long gravel drive to my grandparents' house is already lined with cars when we arrive a few minutes later. There are lots of pickup trucks and large SUVs. People are gathered in the front yard under the big maple tree that shades the lawn. I haven't been to the farm for several years, but it looks pretty much the same. There's a square white clapboard house with a long porch across the front. Wide steps from the center of the porch lead down to the concrete walkway.

The house looks a little sad, though, as no one has lived here for years. The curtains are drawn like shuttered eyelids. There are no containers of the flowers my grandmother loved decorating the stoop. My grandparents moved south when they retired, and now another farmer rents the acreage from them.

My dad and Mr. Clement are standing at the bottom of the steps talking to some of the people gathered on the grass. My younger brother, Drew, is on the porch, leaning back against the railing, reading a book. Some people thought to bring folding chairs and are seated in ragged rows facing the house, chatting amongst themselves. They're neighbors, after all, who probably don't see much of each other during the busy summer months. I'm surprised at how many people have come.

My mom goes over to my dad, gives him a brief hug, and reaches up to pat Drew on the knee. He jumps up and gives her a big hug, then looks embarrassed about it. I know it's hard on him to have all of us away. The rest of the group from the field study migrates toward the edge of the driveway. Zeke and Lorraine sit near the front, but off to the side. I'm hyperaware of them now and feel this need to know where they are at all times so I can covertly observe them.

I take a seat on the grass next to Leo and nudge him in the side. "No heckling."

"Can't I even ask some pointed questions?"

"Only if you're prepared to deal with the answers." I've seen my dad and Mr. Clement in very heated discussions on environmental topics before. They know their stuff and are passionate about it.

My dad checks his watch after he sees the group from the dig has arrived. He turns to Mr. Clement and says something, then gives his attention to the waiting crowd.

"Good morning. Thank you for coming. For those of you who don't know me, I'm Paul Horton. My parents own this farm. Some of you may have known them—Gayle and Leonard Horton."

Some people in the crowd nod and murmur in assent.

"This is Stuart Clement. He's a personal friend and an attorney with Earth Cause. We asked you all here to talk about United

Energy's plans to expand its fracking activity in the area." Dad takes a step back to give the floor to Mr. Clement.

In the quiet, I can hear the breeze rustling through the stalks of corn in the field that borders the yard and in the leaves of the tree overhead. The movement causes the dappled spots of sun and shade on the ground to swirl in a kaleidoscope pattern.

Mr. Clement comes forward. "We know there's been fracking in this part of Indiana on a small scale for years," he says. "What United Energy is proposing now, however, is much different. They'll be coming to each of you and offering you a substantial amount of money for the right to extensively frack new and existing wells on your land. But they won't give you the real story of what it means for your land and your water. We want to give you the real story."

There's more murmuring from the crowd. Everyone's attention is focused on him.

"Fracking involves pumping hundreds of thousands—even millions—of gallons of water mixed with chemicals into existing wells. The water and chemicals are forced into shale rock deep underground. They form cracks in the rock that release natural methane gas. These chemicals are totally unregulated and are often composed of known carcinogens like benzene, toluene, and ethylbenzene, plus others that we don't know about because the companies don't have to disclose what they use."

Another car approaches on the driveway, its tires crunching on the gravel. I glance over my shoulder and see a white van with the United Energy logo emblazoned on the side in blue and red. Leo gives a start beside me. He averts his eyes from me when I turn toward him. The van comes all the way up to the house and parks right where we're sure to see the logo. Two men dressed in jeans and work shirts, looking very much like the farmers gathered on the lawn, step out. Mr. Clement has stopped talking. He and my dad don't look happy about this development.

"Don't let us interrupt," the older of the two men says. "We heard about the meeting and thought we'd stop by."

"This is a private meeting of neighboring farmers," Mr. Clement says.

"Well, we live in the area too." The man extends his arms palms up. His iron-gray hair is swept back from his face, but he doesn't look too much older than my dad.

"Let them stay," someone from the gathered group calls out. "I'd like to hear what they have to say."

"Yeah, let them stay," says a woman seated in a folding chair directly to my right.

"All right. I guess you can stay," my dad says. The older man nods and the two company representatives stay by the van. The younger one sits in the passenger seat with the door ajar.

"OK," Mr. Clement continues. "As I was saying, the chemicals used are totally unregulated. Much of the fracking water is recovered from the wells, but some is left behind and has been found to contaminate well water and underground aquifers. The water that's recovered is transferred to evaporation tanks, where the chemicals are left to evaporate directly into the air. We're talking about poisonous chemicals in the well water that you use in your home and for your livestock and in the air you breathe."

"But don't the energy companies say it's safe? How could they be allowed to do it if it wasn't safe?" demands a heavyset man who looks close to my grandfather's age and is standing near the front.

"It *is* safe," the United Energy representative says. "There's no proof of any harm coming to anyone as a result of fracking. And it helps make America energy independent."

My dad holds up a hand. "I'll give you an opportunity to talk to everyone at the end of the meeting. But it's still our meeting, so please hold your comments until then."

"Got it," the gray-haired man says. "I was just responding to what was being said."

"Did you have anything to do with this?" I hiss at Leo.

He's sitting hunched over and is ducking his head down. "I don't know. Maybe."

"What do you mean 'maybe'?"

"I might've mentioned it to my dad on the phone the other night. He could've called United Energy to tell them about the meeting, but I'm not sure."

I jab him in the ribs with my elbow. "I would say that he did."

"What's going on?" Eric leans in from my other side.

"Leo invited United Energy to the meeting."

"No, I didn't." He's regained some of his composure and looks more defiant now. He lifts his chin in Eric's direction. "My dad may have invited them. Anyway, the farmers have a right to hear what they have to say."

"Not cool, dude." Eric shakes his head. "Not cool."

My dad has turned back to the group to continue. "We could talk about this all day, and it wouldn't be as impactful as hearing it from folks who've actually experienced the results of fracking on their property. We've asked John Kuhn from Pennsylvania to share what's happened on his farm. You'll also hear from a young man from Kansas who lives in an area where there's been extensive fracking. John, why don't you come up now?"

A short, stocky man with a ruddy face comes to stand next to my dad. He looks a little uncomfortable to be in front of the crowd.

"Go ahead and introduce yourself and tell us your story," my dad says to him.

"Hello, everyone." He puts a hand behind his head and rubs his neck. His other hand is shoved into his front pocket. "I'm a farmer like many of you. I live in Bradford County, Pennsylvania. We grow soybeans and wheat, and we have about twenty head of cattle. A little over five years ago, Citizen's Oil and Gas came to town offering to buy the fracking rights to the farmland in the area. Apparently, there's a big shale field in Pennsylvania and New York with natural gas trapped in it." He stops to clear his throat. "They were offering a lot of money, and things were kind of tight for a lot of us. It seemed like a good idea. We'd had oil wells on our property for years without any problems. We didn't know any better, so we took the money and gave them the fracking rights. Now I wish it had never happened."

He looks directly at the two guys from United Energy. He shoves his other hand into his front pocket and rocks back on his heels. The older guy looks like he really wants to say something, but my dad quells him with a look.

"They came in with all of their trucks and equipment and started drilling. One well and some evaporation tanks are only about two hundred yards from our house, which isn't pleasant, but we could live with that. But not long after they started fracking, bad things started happening. We noticed that the water from our well had a bad smell and a bad taste to it. This was the water we drank ourselves and used for our livestock and to irrigate the crops.

"One of our neighbors was certain that methane gas had gotten into our well water. He had the crazy idea to see if the water from our tap would light on fire. I didn't believe him. I thought, 'How could an American company do something like that in our country, to American citizens?' But he was right. The water coming from our tap, from our well, is flammable."

The gathered crowd is silent listening to his story. A bee buzzes by my head, and I shoo it away and shift my position on the grass.

"Then we started getting sick. And our livestock started getting sick. The cows were losing weight and not producing as much milk. I got a rash on my skin that won't go away no matter the amount of ointment from my doctor I use on it." He pushes up his sleeve to show a red, blotchy, scaly rash on his forearm. "My wife developed a cough and feels ill and run down all the time. At first, we didn't connect all this to the fracking. But then some environmental groups came to talk to us. One of the guys had an infrared camera that he used on the evaporation tanks— the tanks that are located next to the well, two hundred yards from my house. He showed us the colorless fumes that were evaporating directly into the air. Toxic chemicals, with names that I don't even know, evaporating right into the air that my family and all my neighbors breathe all day long." His voice cracks a little at this point.

"And we weren't the only ones having problems. Everyone in the area has contaminated water and some sort of health issue." His words are flowing more easily now as he warms to his subject, and his voice gets stronger. "With the help of the environmental groups, we confronted Citizen's Oil and Gas, but they denied that the illnesses had any connections to fracking and denied any responsibility. They said there was no proof that fracking had any-thing to do with it. *No proof!* When we could literally light our tap water on fire!" He takes off his ball cap and slaps it against his leg.

He looks around at the crowd and replaces the cap. "They did agree to truck in cisterns of drinking water for us to use, but on the condition that we wouldn't talk about it. I'm risking my drinking water by coming here, but I don't want what happened to us in Pennsylvania to happen to you. We're also trying to get the state government involved in passing legislation against fracking, but that's an uphill battle too. I'm no politician, but now I know that corporations have a much greater influence on our government than I ever imagined."

He stops and bows his head for a moment. "My farm has been in my family for generations. I have nowhere else to go and nowhere else that I ever wanted to be. It's my life. But now I think it's slowly killing me to stay there. I'm just a farmer like all of you; I'm not a politician and not an environmental activist. I'm here because I want you to know what happened to me because of fracking—so it doesn't happen to you. That's all."

The crowd is visibly moved by his speech. One of the field study students in front of me starts clapping, then everyone is clapping. A few people even stand up. I stand up too. I feel a boiling anger that something like this could happen, that a company would deliberately and knowingly poison people's air and drinking water to make a profit. Mr. Kuhn looks uncomfortable with all the attention, but he takes off his hat and gives a little bow.

Once everyone's settled back down, my dad steps forward again and places his hand on Mr. Kuhn's shoulder. "Thank you, John. We appreciate you coming all this way to share your story." He turns to Scott. "Our second speaker, Scott Smitson, comes from Kansas. He's here working on an archaeological dig with my wife and some colleagues. Go ahead, Scott."

"Hey," Scott says as he waves a hand to the crowd. In contrast to the farmers, he is wearing cargo shorts and a T-shirt and sandals. The sun has moved further overhead and beats down on his blond hair.

"My family's farm is in the southeastern section of Kansas," he says. "We had the same experience as Mr. Kuhn. The energy companies came around and tried to buy the fracking rights on our land. By this time, though, we'd heard some of the stories coming from places like Pennsylvania, so a lot of farmers said no. My family didn't allow them to frack our wells. But there were still a lot of people who did. Those people had the same negative experiences as Mr. Kuhn. I know they also wish they'd never allowed fracking on their land."

I glance over at the two guys from United Energy. I can't tell if this makes them uncomfortable or if they're used to dealing with this sort of stuff.

When Scott started talking, Zeke got up from where he was sitting off to the side and made his way over to where Mr. Kuhn was standing in the shade of the tree. I keep an eye on them as I listen to Scott.

"Instead of repeating what Mr. Kuhn has already shared, I wanted to tell you about another side effect of fracking that we're experiencing in Kansas: earthquakes."

Zeke is shaking hands with Mr. Kuhn. As their hands connect, a soft glow of light moves from Zeke's hand into Mr. Kuhn's hand and up his forearm. While they talk, Zeke puts his hand on Mr. Kuhn's shoulder, then onto his back. Every time Zeke touches Mr. Kuhn, a golden glow of light emanates from his hands and is absorbed by Mr. Kuhn. I'm not sure if Mr. Kuhn notices it, or if anyone else does, for that matter. I look around, but most people are paying attention to Scott.

"Hey," I whisper as I nudge Eric with my elbow. "Look over at Zeke and Mr. Kuhn. Do you see anything strange?"

"Maybe. I'm not sure. Yeah, I do see something. Mr. Kuhn is shining."

"Do you see the light coming from Zeke's hands?"

He squints at Zeke. "Yeah, now I see it. What the hell? What is he doing?"

"I have no idea. Some sort of weird healing technique, maybe? Can they do that too?"

"Who knows? They seem to be able to do all kinds of crazy things."

"What are you talking about?" Renee whispers as she leans over.

Eric tells her about the light coming from Zeke's hands and how Mr. Kuhn shining.

"I don't see anything," she says. "Are you sure you're seeing light coming from his hands? Maybe it's just a reflection or something."

"No, there's definitely a glow around Mr. Kuhn. I'm sure of it," I say.

Zeke gives Mr. Kuhn's hand a final shake and turns away. He looks directly at us, and the corner of his mouth quirks into a smile. *He knows we saw the light.* I'll have to ask him about it later. He sits back down in the row in front of me, and I turn my attention back to Scott.

"After they began fracking extensively in our part of the state, we started having a lot of seismic activity—earthquakes. Not big ones, but lots of smaller ones. This is in an area that doesn't have any fault lines. We didn't experience much earthquake activity before the fracking started. Even though the quakes aren't large, we can feel a lot of them."

Scott slams his fist into the palm of his other hand. "They're messing with the geology of the area! I'm minoring in geology, so I know what I'm talking about here. The water they pump into the ground is intended to break apart the rock to release

TRACY RICHARDSON

trapped natural gas. What it also seems to be doing is undermining the stability of the bedrock. They pump millions of gallons of water into the ground to extract the gas. They remove the chemical-laden water, and a lot of it is pumped right back into the ground, into wastewater wells. Scientists say there's a connection between fracking and the increase in earthquakes, but the energy companies deny it. Just like they deny responsibility for everything else."

This is news to me. I had no idea that fracking caused earthquakes. It's hard to understand why anyone would allow fracking on their land given the negative consequences. I get why Scott is so passionate about it.

"In Kansas we're not near a major fault, but in southern Indiana you are." He points to the assembled crowd. "You're smack in between the Wabash Valley Seismic Zone and the New Madrid Fault Line. Messing with the geology here could have major consequences." He brings his hands down to his sides and looks over at my dad. "That's all I have to say. Thanks for giving me a chance to talk."

A couple of the guys from the dig call out whoops of encouragement, and Scott receives a round of applause as well.

"I can't believe that fracking can also cause earthquakes," Renee says. "There seems to be nothing good about it."

"Except the money it makes the energy companies," I say.

"And the clean, affordable energy it generates," Leo says.

I glare at him.

An older, heavyset man toward the front of the crowd says, "Let's hear what United Energy has to say." Several others reiterate his request.

"OK." My dad extends his arm toward the guys from United Energy. "It's your turn."

The younger of the two men hops down from where he was sitting in the front seat of their van. The two of them walk over to stand on the sidewalk in front of the crowd. The older man smiles broadly and faces the gathered farmers.

"Well, after hearing all of that, I can completely understand why you would be concerned. United Energy is also concerned about you—and about America. We take these claims very seriously and have done extensive research on the effects of fracking. So have many government agencies. We wouldn't want to do anything that would cause any harm to our citizens." He brings his fist to his chest over his heart and gazes out over the crowd. He's walking back and forth in front of the group, speaking in a loud and commanding voice. He reminds me a bit of a preacher giving a sermon.

"Those studies have not found any conclusive connections between fracking and health issues or earthquakes." He shakes his index finger in the air. "Not one. If it was harmful in any way, we wouldn't do it. We wouldn't be allowed to do it."

This is such a load of bull that I can't even believe he's saying it, but I see some of the farmers in the crowd nodding their heads in agreement.

"See?" Leo whispers in my ear. "It's completely safe."

"You are totally delusional," I answer back. "Of course they're going to lie. It makes them way too much money."

The United Energy guy is still talking. "What fracking does do is help America and Americans. It lowers the cost of natural gas. It also allows us to be energy independent, so we don't have to rely on the Middle East for oil. Fracking is good for America." He stops walking again and smiles. "It'll also put some money in your pocket, which I know would be welcome to many of you. Am I right?" He cocks an eyebrow at a middle-aged woman sitting near the front, and she nods her head in agreement. The crowd murmurs its assent.

"The beautiful thing about our country is that you get to decide for yourself what you want to do with your land. We'll be contacting each of you individually to go over our offers, and you can decide what is best for you. My name is Stuart Houseman, and this is my colleague Brice Fletcher." He motions to the younger man standing off to one side. "Both of us will stick around for a while to answer any questions you might have. Thank you for your time." He walks over and shakes hands with my dad and Mr. Clement, which seems to take them by surprise.

The crowd dissolves into conversation, and the meeting is effectively over. I think my dad may have wanted to say some closing words, but he's lost everyone's attention. They're getting up from their chairs and talking in small groups.

"I'm going to go over to say hi to Dad and Drew," I tell Leo, Renee, and Eric. On my way past, I tap Scott on the shoulder, and he looks up at me. "That was great, what you had to say. Thanks."

"It's just the truth," he says. "Which is more than I can say for what the United Energy guy told everyone. I hope it helps."

"Me too."

Drew sees me walking over and runs up to say hello.

"Hey, buddy," I say and box him a few shots on the arm. "Are you holding down the fort at home?"

"I had soccer camp last week." He gets in a few punches of his own to my gut. "I made three goals in scrimmage."

"That's great!" I say. "You're an awesome striker."

My dad comes over to where we're standing and ruffles Drew's hair. "We've got another soccer star in the family."

"Hey, Dad. That was a great meeting. Having Mr. Kuhn and Scott talk was brilliant. It sucks that United Energy showed up. That guy seemed like such a sleaze to me, but I saw a lot of people nodding in agreement with him."

"Unfortunately, there will be some people who believe that the energy companies really do have their best interests at heart. It's hard to accept that a company would knowingly do something harmful in the name of profit."

"What happens next?" I'm trying not to feel discouraged. Fighting a huge corporation like United Energy seems like a daunting and impossible task.

"We keep fighting. This is only the beginning," he says.

I wish I shared his confidence.

Several people have come up to talk with my dad. I look around for Leo. He's over talking with the group around United Energy. I really like Leo, but his continued support of fracking, especially in light of what Zeke and Lorraine showed us, could be a deal breaker.

10

"Zeke, wait up," I call as I get out of the car back at the dormitory compound. He's walking over the grassy area toward the staff dorms. He stops and turns toward me.

"Do you have a minute? Maybe there's somewhere we could go to talk that's more private?" I ask as I jog over to him.

"Sure," Zeke says. I hadn't really thought about it before, but Zeke's sharp cheekbones, aquiline nose, and dark hair hint at a Native American background. His blue-gray eyes stand out in contrast. "There's a small stream that runs behind the staff dorms where we can sit on some logs on the bank. I thought you might have questions." He turns back toward the path to the staff dorm. "Come. You'll like this spot. The water is especially soothing and rhythmic."

We walk toward the squat tan building that is a replica of the guys' dorm. Behind it is an open area that slopes gently down to a stream I can hear before I see it. The water is splashing over rocks, and there's a small waterfall over some fallen branches. Zeke folds his lanky body to sit on a moss-covered log that lies rotting on the shore and motions for me to join him.

"What are your questions?" He looks at me expectantly.

I'm a little nervous about this, but not because of anything Zeke is doing. In fact, I feel a strong sense of calm acceptance from him.

"Well, the first one is about Leo." I find I can't look Zeke in the eye. This feels so personal because of my feelings for Leo. "Why are you including him in the meditations when he's so resistant to it and basically a climate change denier? I mean, I like Leo and all, but it doesn't make sense."

"My child." Zeke places his hand under my chin and lifts my face so I'm looking him in the eye. "Things are always more complicated than they seem." He tilts his head to one side and raises his hand up, palm toward the sky. "Leo is very conflicted. He's been taught one thing by his father and now he's being presented with evidence to contradict what he was told. As events unfold, Leo will have a role to play. That's all I can say for now."

"OK. I get being confused. It's a lot to take in. Except that it's so obvious that fracking is bad." Zeke nods in agreement. I move to the next question.

"I'm also wondering about something that happened at the meeting this morning. When you were talking with Mr. Kuhn, Eric and I thought we saw a light coming from your hands." I hesitate and look at my own hands, resting in my lap, then at Zeke's hands. "What was that?"

"I was giving him healing light energy to alleviate the illnesses he contracted from the chemicals in the water and air at his home."

"I could see a glowing light, but Renee didn't see it. I don't think anyone else could either, or at least they didn't notice. Why is that?"

"Being able to see higher vibrational energy is a combination of two factors." He draws two parallel lines in the dirt at our feet with a stick. "The first is the vibrational frequency of the observer." He draws a zigzag down the center of the line on the left. "The second is the desire of the higher-vibrating person to be seen." He draws a circle around the line on the right. "You and your brother are vibrating at a higher frequency, and so you could see the healing light. Also, I didn't want everyone to see it, so they didn't."

"What does that mean—that we are vibrating at a higher frequency? And why would we see it and not the others?" My hands are feeling clammy, so I rub them against my shorts.

"Your experience connecting with the spirit of the Native American girl at your lake house opened you up to higher vibrations. As your scientists are beginning to discover, everything is made up of energy. Thoughts are also energy, powerful energy. When you raise the vibration of your consciousness, you're able to connect with higher energy levels, such as Fifth Dimensional energy." He draws a third and fourth line in the dirt horizontally across the top of the other two lines.

"The Fifth Dimension?" I ask. "Are you and Lorraine in the Fifth Dimension? Is that why you have these abilities?"

"Yes. Earth and most of its inhabitants are currently in the Third Dimension. There are many higher dimensions in the universe. We're here to help you ascend to the Fifth Dimension so you can help others."

Holy shit. I wanted to know what the mission was, but this is crazy. Ascend to the Fifth Dimension? What does that even mean? Apprehension washes over me, and I wonder yet again if I want to be part of this.

"How do we do that—raise our consciousness?"

"We can try it now, if you like. I can help you use your thought energy more intentionally."

"OK, I guess so," I say, not sure if I really want to. I toss a stone I'd been holding into the stream. It lands with a plunk and a splash.

"Begin by breathing rhythmically and quieting your thoughts. It often helps if you close your eyes, but for this exercise I want you to keep your eyes open. I want you to focus on that log over on the bank of the creek." He indicates a log about two feet long and twelve inches around. It's a few feet away.

"All right." Nervousness makes my voice catch, but I breathe out like he instructed.

"Focus your thoughts. Imagine lifting your object into the air with your thoughts. You can do this."

I'm not sure if it's really true, but I'm not about to contradict him.

"Imagine the energy field around your body vibrating at four times the rate of your heartbeat, ta-ta-ta-ta-ta-ta." The words are fast and staccato. "As your vibrational energy increases, you're able to connect with Fifth Dimensional energy and elevate your spiritual consciousness. You can use that energy to move objects." He continues sounding the rapid ta-ta-ta pattern.

I imagine the energy that fills the space around my body pulsing faster and faster in time with his rhythm. I give my attention to the log. I feel a shift, and an unfamiliar feeling of power surges through me. The log moves slightly, but I can't focus enough to make it do anything more. Then I feel Zeke's thoughts combine with mine almost imperceptibly, and a sudden burst of power surges from my mind to the log. It rises about an inch into the air.

I moved it using only my thoughts!

My euphoria is short lived, however. I lose my concentration, and the log falls to the ground and rolls into the creek with a splash. But I did move it. Even if Zeke had to help me along a bit.

"Wow," is all I can manage to say.

"Well done. You're learning quickly. The more you practice, the better you'll become." Zeke smiles broadly, and his eyes crinkle at the corners. "Tonight, on Emerald Mound, Lorraine and I will show you more. Then you'll teach other young people. It's part of your mission in this Earth lifetime. You will teach others, raising both your consciousness and theirs."

A panicky feeling overwhelms me. *I don't want this responsibility.*

I'm sure Zeke can sense my resistance because he says in a firm voice, "Marcie, this is what you came here to do, and you will be able to do it. You have to trust yourself." He places a hand on my shoulder, communicating a sense of calm. "There are millions of young people who want to connect with higher vibrational energy, who want to make a positive impact, but don't know how. You will teach them."

I take a deep breath and lean back on the log, some of the panic dissipating.

I point to the two horizontal lines in Zeke's diagram. "Do those other two lines represent higher energy levels? Are there higher levels than the Fifth Dimension? And is that the explanation for Dark Energy? Is it other dimensions that we can't see?"

I've asked these questions before, discussing them with my dad, who's an amateur astronomy buff. Even if I'm uncertain of how committed I am to this mission, it's fascinating to talk to someone who can answer my questions.

"Yes, there are many higher dimensions. They're not in a different place, but rather exist concurrently with one another. The Dark Energy that your scientists can detect but can't see is the energy of higher realms." He extends his legs out in front of him and arches his back and neck in a long stretch. "We'll talk more about it tonight on Emerald Mound."

He gets up off the log and extends a hand to pull me up. "My stomach is telling me that it's lunchtime. Let's go eat."

11

A BUNCH OF us decide to go into town that afternoon. Leo stays back. In his words, "Shopping's not my thing." Renee, Lainey, and I want to check out a thrift store and a flea market, while Scott and Eric want to visit the music store. We agree to meet up at the coffee shop in a couple hours.

After several enjoyable hours of shopping, Lainey pushes open the door of the coffee shop. "That was fun!"

"We got some great stuff," Renee says.

I spot Eric and Scott pulling out chairs at a circular table in the corner. "The guys are already here," I say. We tuck our packages on the floor under the table.

"Have you ordered yet?" I ask. Renee gives Eric a kiss on both cheeks—one of her very French habits.

"No, we just got here," Scott says. "We can all go up together."

There are three guys in line ahead of us at the counter. One of them turns around and says to Eric, "Hey, weren't you at the meeting this morning where United Energy showed up?"

"Yeah, I was," Eric says. At first I think the guy wants to talk about how bad fracking is. When I take in his aggressive stance and the hostility in his eyes, that idea quickly fades.

"Why don't you and your family just stay up north where you belong and stop poking your noses into our business." He steps toward Eric menacingly. He's a big guy, burly and muscular and probably used to intimidating people, but Eric tops him by a good four inches.

Eric stiffens and holds his hands up in a conciliatory gesture, but his voice is taut when he says, "This *is* our business. We own property here just like the rest of you, and we're concerned about how fracking would affect our land and water. Didn't you hear what the guys from Pennsylvania and Kansas said happened to them?"

The two other local guys move up to flank the one arguing. "I heard it. And I also heard what United Energy said about it being safe." He shoves Eric's shoulder.

Eric is visibly angry but doesn't retaliate. Renee puts her hand on his arm. He brushes it off and maneuvers himself in front of her. Scott steps forward beside Eric. I resist the urge to push past him, to try and stop a fight from breaking out. A fistfight will not help our cause.

"Everything OK here?" Scott asks.

"You're the guy from Kansas who talked at the meeting this morning."

"Yup, that's right."

"I was just telling him." He jabs Eric in the shoulder again. "And now I'll tell you. Stay out of our business. Go back home to Kansas. Fracking is good for America and good for southern Indiana. We won't have to depend on those Arab Muslims for oil, and it'll bring money into the area."

"You don't know what you're talking about," Scott shoots back. "I do. It's a mistake to let them frack on your land." Now the guy shoves Scott hard enough that he loses his balance and stumbles backward.

"Hey! That's enough." Eric puts his hands on the guy's chest.

"Who the hell are you to come down here and tell us what to do?" He pulls back his fist and lands a hard right hook into Eric's face, snapping his head back.

Eric grabs him by the front of the shirt and shoves him hard up against the counter. The glass of the display case rattles from the impact.

A middle-aged woman in an apron comes running over and forces herself between them. "Stop this right now!" She pushes them apart, and Eric relinquishes his hold on the guy's shirt. "Robby, you and your friends need to leave. We don't want any trouble here."

He turns to look somewhat sheepishly at her. "I'm sorry, Mrs. Gebhart." He bares his teeth in a fierce smile. "The trouble started when this guy and his family came down here trying to tell us what we should do on our own land. We'll go—we're not staying."

He turns back to us. "Just remember what I said. Go home."

I bite back the retort on the tip of my tongue and unclench my balled fists, although I'd really like to punch him myself.

"Sorry, ma'am," Eric says after they've gone. "We didn't mean to cause any trouble."

"That may be true, young man, but I think it's too late for that." She places her hands on her hips. "I was at the fracking meeting this morning too. Besides owning this coffee shop, my husband farms forty acres outside of town. I don't want fracking here any more than you do, but there are more than a few people who feel the same way as Robby and his friends. This could get ugly."

I look around the coffee shop. People have stopped gawking at us, but I wonder what all of them are thinking. How many of them would agree with us?

Her demeanor softens. "Let me get you all drinks on the house. Not everyone in town feels the way Robby and his friends do. I'm sorry this happened to you." She pats Eric's shoulder. "I'll get you some ice for your eye."

"That was intense," Scott says when we're seated at our table.

I'm a little uncomfortable staying in the coffee shop, but I don't want to let Robby and his ilk scare us off. Now that the incident is over, I have a slightly sick feeling in my stomach. You try and do something good, to inform and *help* people, and you get punched in the face for it.

"Thanks for stepping up in my moment of need, but I think I could have taken him," Eric says, putting on the bravado, cracking his knuckles and trying to lighten the mood.

Scott laughs. "Maybe you could have taken Robby, but that would leave me to deal with the other two guys. Unless the girls decided to join in."

I roll my eyes at him.

"Seriously, though, I wasn't expecting anything like that to happen. He was totally hostile. I can't believe he actually hit me." He places the bag of ice Mrs. Gebhart gave him against his face and winces.

"You'll probably have a black eye to show for it," I say. "Mom's gonna love that."

"Great. I'm not looking forward to that conversation."

"Things can get pretty tense around the whole fracking debate," Scott says. "It happened back home. Maybe I should have warned you and your dad." He rubs his hand along his jaw. "Sometimes I wonder if it's even worth it, after all the grief you get from the energy companies and the people who just want to make a quick load of cash. But I've seen the same issues that Mr. Kuhn described affect my neighbors. These companies knowingly pollute our water and contaminate our land for profit, so we have to fight."

"You couldn't have known it would get hostile here . . . and so quickly," I say.

We're silent a moment as we sip our drinks.

"Why would he care enough to start a fight?" Lainey asks.

"Some people don't like it when they feel like other people are meddling in their business, I guess. He really seemed to consider us outsiders. Then there was what he said about Arabs and Muslims. Sometimes reactions like that are based on fear disguised as hate," I say.

Just like how Zeke and Lorraine described it: fear versus love. I know which side I'm on.

12

As it turns out, I don't go to pick up Leo at the guys' dorm to go Emerald Mound that night. After dinner someone started a bonfire, and everyone who didn't go out for the evening is gathered around the fire making s'mores and hanging out. We're waiting until dark to go to the mound.

Leo and I are toasting marshmallows for our own s'mores. He likes his burnt to a crisp; I don't want mine to burn. I like it golden brown on the outside and hot and gooey on the inside to perfectly melt the chocolate in the s'more without giving it a burned charcoal taste.

Mr. Clement went home after the fracking meeting, but my dad and Drew are staying the night. Drew is over the moon because he'll be sleeping on a cot in Eric's room. My dad is staying with my mom in the staff dorm. Drew is sitting between Eric and Leo. Renee went up to her room after dinner to put away the stuff she bought that afternoon. Drew's pretty much in boy heaven, if that's a place. It's nice to have my family all together.

"Did you get a feel for which way people were leaning after the meeting this morning?" my mom asks my dad.

"Stuart and I hung around afterwards and talked to a bunch of people, but so did the guys from United Energy. There are certainly a fair number who are against fracking and understand the risks associated with it." My dad looks over to where Eric is sitting. His eyelid is puffed almost completely closed, and the skin is turning a dark shade of purple. "I'd say we can be pretty sure there're an equal number who were swayed by the United Energy storyline, given what we heard after the meeting and what happened to Eric today."

I lean forward so I can add to the conversation. "I don't get it. How can anyone want fracking on their land after hearing what Scott and Mr. Kuhn had to say?"

"It's complicated, honey." Firelight glints off my dad's glasses. "A lot of people are distrustful of what they consider 'so-called' science. Plenty don't even believe that human activity has a real impact on the Earth."

"The energy companies also do a really good job of disseminating propaganda that promotes natural gas as the new 'clean energy' and wraps it in patriotism. It plays into the whole issue of American dependence on foreign oil," my mom adds.

"Natural gas is the future of energy in America. You'll see," Leo says.

No one replies. We just leave his statement hanging in the air, unsupported and alone.

Scott chimes in as if Leo hadn't spoken. "There are so many better energy alternatives. In Reykjavík, Iceland, they use geothermal and hydroelectric energy sources almost exclusively. Then there's solar and wind, which are both totally renewable and truly clean."

And what about the energy in the Unified Field? I saw what it could do on Greystone Mountain.

"That's true," my dad says in reply to Scott, "but a lot of US energy policy is driven by corporations, and corporations are driven by profit. Clean energy just isn't as profitable to the energy companies as fossil fuels. And it requires a fundamental change in business that many people and corporations aren't willing to make."

"It's just so frustrating," I say.

"I think our side will prevail in the end." My mom has taken off her hat and let her hair down. It's almost the same strawberry-blond color as mine, with only a few stray gray strands running through it.

"We'll have to," my dad says. "The alternative is destruction."

The images of charred trees and barren ground from the vision Zeke gave us on the mountain flash into my head. I hope my parents are right.

Around 9:15, Eric gets up and tells Drew he's going to find Renee but will be back in time for bed. Leo and I wait a few minutes before we excuse ourselves from the group at the bonfire to go to Emerald Mound.

The moon is almost full. After our eyes adjust to the darkness, we can easily see by its light and the light of the stars to walk across the field without using a flashlight. The others are gathered at the base of the mound when Leo and I arrive.

Lorraine and Zeke lead us up a path worn between the swathes of tall grass that cover the mound. It winds around the sides of the hill, encircling it almost like a maze or labyrinth. Leo's flip-flops thwap against the hard-packed earth of the path as we ascend.

"How's the other guy look?" Leo asks Eric.

Eric reaches up to touch his eye and winces. "I didn't hit him. Not that I didn't want to. I'd shoved him up against the counter when the coffee shop owner came running over and made him and his friends leave." He shrugs. "It's probably a good thing."

"Yeah, for sure," Leo says. "I'm surprised he was ready to fight you. I mean . . . over fracking."

"When he asked if I was at the meeting this morning, I thought at first that he wanted to talk about how bad fracking is. I wasn't expecting him to be so hostile."

"People don't like being told what to do," Renee interjects.

"I guess," Eric says. He turns back to Leo. "You decided to come tonight. I wasn't sure you would."

"I wasn't sure either, but Marcie more or less convinced me that I should." Leo smiles at me and squeezes my hand. I feel a hot blush creeping up my neck.

"There's a lot of research on the benefits of meditation." Why do I feel like I have to defend it to him? "It may not be your thing."

"Yeah, that's what I'm thinking," he says.

By this time we've wound our way around to the top of the mound. It's a flat area about the size of a basketball court, but more rounded. The open space follows the shape of the mound, with the grass mown short. If it were light out, then we'd have a nice view back toward Angel Mound and the village area we're excavating. But I don't think we could see over the treetops in the other direction to the river.

Zeke stops at about the center point of the open area. Moonlight casts his long, thin shadow so it looks like the arm of a clock as we gather in a loose circle around him. He lays down his pack and removes a small brass bowl and wooden mallet from it. He places these items on the ground in front of him, lights a camp lantern, and places it in the center of the circle.

"At one time there was a wooden henge here on the top of Emerald Mound. The people who lived here used it to track the movements of the sun and moon and other celestial objects and events, including the solstices and equinoxes. They were very aware of the movement of the stars and how this affects life on Earth. We'll be using the energy that remains here to amplify our meditation tonight."

Not too weird so far. I shift around to settle myself in the grass.

Lorraine stands opposite Zeke. She raises her hands, the gesture encompassing all of us in the circle. "Tonight we'll be teaching you a technique called *pulsing*, in which you'll learn to increase the frequency of your energy body, resulting in *shimmering* and a raising of your vibration. When you're *shimmering,* you will be physically moving between the dimensions. This is in preparation for ascension to the Fifth Dimension. We'll also lead you in a healing meditation on the aura of the Earth."

Leo raises his eyebrows and cocks his head to one side. I shrug in response.

Lorraine lowers herself to the ground. She's wearing her hair down and it falls loosely around her shoulders, glowing golden in the moonlight. "Don't be concerned if what you see and feel is different from what another experiences. You are all on your own paths."

I just hope Leo's experience tonight is good. I feel somehow responsible.

"Zeke will begin by raising our vibration, then I'll guide you through the meditation. Is everyone ready? Any questions?"

I glance around at the others, their faces showing different degrees of expectation and apprehension. No one says anything.

"All right. Let's begin." Lorraine closes her eyes and tilts her face toward the sky.

I do the same.

Zeke begins speaking slowly and rhythmically in a language I don't understand but possibly recognize. Maybe it's Hebrew or Greek. There are a few words I catch: Adonai and Yahweh and Kadoosh.

Zeke's deep voice is smooth and musical; the sound swirls around and through me, filling the night air with a palpable current of sound. After a few minutes his words change to something truly foreign, alien in every sense of the word. I find that—although I don't understand the words—the meaning of what he is chanting reaches my very core. It's about universal love and connectedness. My thoughts begin to fade away, and I have a sense of just being, joining with the sound of his voice.

Now Zeke's chanting becomes softer, fading into the background as Lorraine begins speaking.

"Imagine your energy field, your aura, extending a foot or two beyond your physical body. This is your energy body. It glows and pulsates with colors representing your seven chakras or energy centers."

I try to imagine a field of energy surrounding me. I see orange and green and blue light swirling around me. Zeke's chanting is low and reassuring.

"Think of it as your cosmic egg, surrounding you and protecting you. Negative influences such as radiation, pollution, and attacks from lower vibrational beings can cause tears to occur in your aura. To protect yourself and heal your aura, visualize that it is surrounded by a purple ring of light shielding you from negative influences and repairing any damage to your cosmic egg. This is powerful divine protection."

I picture the energy field surrounding me being enveloped in a layer of deep purple light. In my mind's eye, I see tears and rough spots in my aura. I envision them closing up and smooth-ing over. As I repair my aura, I begin to feel better. A profound sense of well-being envelops me.

"Now focus on the vibration of your aura," Lorraine says. "It's vibrating at a certain frequency or speed. Concentrate on accelerating the speed of your vibration."

Zeke's chanting changes to the rapid ta-ta-ta-ta-ta he used by the stream. Although I'm aware of what Zeke and Lorraine are saying and following her instructions, I'm in a deeply meditative state at this point. Part of me is still aware of what's going on around me, though, like a detached observer.

I try to match the pulsing of my aura to the rhythm of Zeke's chanting. I sense an almost audible hum in the vibration sur-rounding me. Several minutes pass as Zeke chants the staccato sound. Lorraine's clear, strong voice is a herald calling me to continue with the meditation.

"I am sending a column of blue and gold Fifth Dimensional light. It surrounds all of us gathered in this circle. I want you to envision your energy body rising up the column of light until you are above the Earth plane and can see Earth below. As we rise, we will pass through the Fourth Dimension, but you are protected from negative energy. We have asked our guides and the Ascended Masters for protection."

I see the column of light and begin to ascend through it, encased in my cosmic egg. Outside the corridor I sense dark energy and fear and a palpable malevolence. It pulls on me as if urging me to move out of the corridor, ripping at the serenity of my meditation with promises of power and wealth. Fingers of fear and doubt travel up my spine. Undefined shapes and faceless creatures undulate and shift just beyond the safety of the light. There's a sudden flash of bright light, an explosion of blue and gold and white, growing larger and larger. It obliterates the darkness and disperses the creatures within it. As I continue to move up the column of light, the fear and malevolence recede and are replaced with feelings of joy and love. I've entered the Fifth Dimension.

My whole being is thrumming like a stringed instrument. I have so much energy pulsing through me it almost feels like I'm hovering slightly above the ground. Swirls of blue and gold light envelop me. I also have a sense of the others, the ancient Native spirits, surrounding us. I felt them when we first arrived at the base of Emerald Mound this evening. Their connection with Earth is strong and deep, and now they're combining their energy with ours to magnify the power of our meditation. They dance outside the circle we've formed, chanting in concert with Zeke. I focus on Lorraine's voice as my guide.

"We have passed through the Fourth Dimension into the Fifth," Lorraine says. "See Earth below you now. Earth is a conscious living being, as is everything in the universe. This is a critical juncture for Earth. A great dichotomy is occurring. Many are exploiting Earth for her resources. Influences from the lower vibrations of the Fourth Dimension are fueling greed and lust for power with no regard for the consequences to Earth's stability. It's nearing the tipping point, where she will no longer be able to absorb and recover from the abuse. Fortunately, it is also a time of great spiritual awakening on Earth. People such as yourselves are becoming aware of the complexities of the multidimensional universe and connecting with Divine Source energy. Earth needs our help to heal so she, too, can ascend to the higher spiritual realm of the Fifth Dimension.

"Look closely at the aura that surrounds Earth and you'll see the rips where her energy is leaking. Look to Russia, where the

Chernobyl nuclear reactor meltdown occurred. Look to Japan, where the WWII bombs were dropped, and another nuclear reactor is leaking radiation."

Earth is a beautiful blue jewel suspended in the cosmos below me. Swirls of white clouds drift over her surface. Beyond that, surrounding the entire Earth, is a golden layer of energy. As I locate Russia, I can see that a stream of golden light is leaking out of the aura into the darkness of space. In fact, the golden aura appears to be leaking in many places, some worse than others. There are so many! What can we do?

Lorraine answers my unasked question. "We can help by joining together and sending healing thought energy to Earth. Focus your thoughts on sending balancing and harmonious energy to Gaia, Mother Earth. There is power in our combined thought energy. Silently meditate on balance and healing for Earth."

Zeke has stopped chanting, and I hear the rich bell tones of the singing bowl he brought with him. The Native spirits also stop chanting; they are now playing drums in accompaniment to Zeke's bowl. The two concentric circles made up of our group and the Native people form a torus of powerful thought energy flowing around us and into the column of light surrounding us. We are connected to Earth and connected to the Fifth Dimension, bringing healing to Earth.

After a few minutes, Lorraine speaks again. "Now see in your mind's eye how the Earth is covered with a grid of lines. These are the ley lines, the energy grid of the Earth. Many sacred sites are located along the ley lines, including the pyramids in Egypt, the Mayan temples in the Yucatán Peninsula, Stonehenge in England, and Serpent Mound in Ohio. They are connected to one another, amplifying each other's power. Human activity, such as fracking or the underground detonation of nuclear bombs, can disrupt these energy meridians."

I am still in my cosmic egg in the blue-gold light corridor. I no longer see the dancing spirits, but I continue to feel their presence. As I move my attention from Earth's aura to the ley lines, I see that they look almost like the latitude and longitude lines on a globe, crisscrossing the planet—except they are much more irregular, not evenly spaced or parallel. Some lines appear less distinct than others, and some seem to be broken in places.

"Our meditation will also serve to strengthen Earth's ley lines," Lorraine says.

The sound of Zeke's bowl fills the air with music, ringing clear and strong. I focus on sending love and light to Earth. I'm not sure how much time passes.

Lorraine's voice continues to guide us. "Now we will return to our Third Dimension bodies. Slowly move back through the corridor of light, through the Fourth Dimension and back to the top of Emerald Mound. Connect to Earth to ground your energy. When you are ready, you can open your eyes."

The drumming changes to a slow, resonant tempo, and I feel my vibration slow as I focus on connecting with the Earth. The feeling of connectedness and of being beyond space and time are still with me as I leave the Fifth Dimension, but there is also sadness in knowing that I can't stay there yet.

My awareness settles back into my physical self, seated on the grass on the top of the mound. I take a deep breath and open my eyes. Leo is looking back and forth from Zeke and Lorraine to the rest of us as if he can't quite figure out what's just happened.

"Wow," I say. My body is still thrumming with the vibrations of sound and light.

"Would anyone like to share what they experienced?" Lorraine asks.

"I'm wondering about the Fourth Dimension," Renee says. Her voice quavers. "It felt very heavy, negative, and frightening. What was that?"

"There are beings in the Fourth Dimension who are not connecting to Spirit," Zeke answers. "Those beings wish to control Third Dimension activities for their own power or gain. Many of the problems now occurring on Earth are a result of Fourth Dimension influence." The memory of the fear and malevolence I felt there is still with me, but it can't reach me through my protective energy field.

"I felt the negative presence." Eric's holding Renee's hand and has scooted closer to her. "But I saw the light too. And Earth's aura."

"So did I," Leo says, sounding surprised.

"Can our meditation really help heal the Earth?" Renee asks.

"I'd like to know that too. It seems pretty outlandish for our thoughts to have any impact on nuclear radiation or catastrophes on the Earth," Leo says.

"Thought energy is the most powerful and fastest energy in the universe," Zeke says. "Its power is exponentially increased when joined together with similar thoughts. The Universal Energy Field is composed of all the thoughts of humankind. If enough people focus on thoughts of healing Earth and creating peace and harmony, it can have a tremendous impact. Our scientists have shown that to be true in their studies of the power of prayer and thought projection."

"I've been working on experiments with Renee's father. He's a physicist." Eric glances at Renee, but she keeps her eyes on the ground. "We're trying to connect to the Universal Energy

Field, and we've had some success with it. Our theory is that the Field can be tapped into as an unlimited energy source . . . and that it's also somehow our connection to each other and . . ." He hesitates, rubbing his hand across the back of his neck. "And to God."

"Yes," Zeke answers. "We are all connected to each other and to the Divine Source, or what you might call God, through our thoughts."

Leo stands up, his body tense with an emotion I can't identify. "If that's true, then why doesn't our government fund research for it? An unlimited source would solve all of our energy problems." He looks down at me. "My dad works for the Department of Energy. He would know about something like this. He would have told me. This is bullshit. Science fiction."

"I can tell you why," Eric says. "If energy were freely available in the space around us, then energy companies couldn't charge for it or control it. No corporation or government would reveal that kind of discovery."

Leo looks between me and Eric and sits abruptly back down on the grass. "I don't believe any of this. Government cover-ups . . . thought energy saving the world? Come on!" Then, quietly, so only I can hear, he says, "Sorry, I just don't buy it."

My happiness dims a little. How can it be so clear to me and not to him?

13

"I think I'm going to take off now," Leo says. "By myself." He gives me a pained look. "I hope you understand."

I don't really understand, but I muster a weak smile. "Sure, I'll see you later."

"Are you OK, babe?" Eric asks Renee.

I can feel her vibrating with anxiety. The experience of passing through the Fourth Dimension was pretty frightening.

"Not really," she says in a small voice. "Do you mind if we leave too?" She looks apprehensively at Zeke and Lorraine.

"OK." Eric stands and pulls her up with him. He looks like he'd really like to stay and talk to Zeke and Lorraine, but not if it means upsetting Renee. "I think we're going to go back too," he tells us.

Zeke gets up from the grass and comes to stand beside Renee. He reaches to put his hand on her arm, and she flinches slightly but doesn't turn away. When he touches her, I see a glow of light move from his hand into her arm—the same glow that I saw when he healed Mr. Kuhn that morning. Renee relaxes at his touch.

"Dear one," Zeke says as the light flows across the skin of her arm and over her entire body. "You are protected. You have nothing to fear. It is your own fear that leaves you open to the psychic attacks of Fourth Dimension beings, but they cannot harm you unless you allow it. If you trust in your own strength and power, your fear will fall away."

Renee stares at him open mouthed for a moment, then stiffens. Her posture becomes rigid.

"It's not easy to accept that we create our own reality," he says.

"How can you say that to me?" she exclaims. "That it's somehow my fault the Fourth Dimension beings affect me. Is it also my fault that I don't connect to the Field?" Angry tears course down her face, and she wipes them away. "What did you see?" she challenges Eric, her fists clenched by her sides.

"I saw what you did." He reaches for her, but she jerks away.

I'm pretty sure this isn't a good time to mention that I saw the Native guides dancing around us.

"It's not a contest," he says. "It's OK if we all have different experiences."

"My experience was so awful." Renee's face crumples, the tears flowing freely now. This time when Eric reaches for her, she lets him pull her into an embrace. "They were all around me, almost taunting me. Even when the light came, and they disappeared, I was still so afraid that I couldn't focus on the rest of the meditation. I didn't see Earth's aura, or the ley lines, or anything," she says between sobs and gulps of air. "What am I doing wrong?"

"You're not doing anything wrong," Lorraine says. "That's not what Zeke meant. It's a learning process, to focus your thoughts. You know you can connect. You've done it in the experiments in your father's lab and when you're in the flow with your art."

"I've seen you do it." Eric strokes her hair.

"I can do the remote viewing," she says with a little more confidence. "Maybe not as much as you, but I do connect with the Field. I'm very intuitive." She sniffs.

"Yes, you are. You're extremely creative and intuitive. It's how you connect to Spirit," Zeke says. "What about you, Marcie? What did you experience?"

I hesitate. I don't want to upset Renee any further. "I felt the Fourth Dimension. It was evil and menacing, but the blue and gold light swept it away. I did see the aura of the Earth and the ley lines."

A breeze picks up, rustling the grasses on the hillside and making the light from the lantern flicker.

"I'm really concerned about the images you showed us last time of the destruction of the Earth. Can we really change that with our thoughts? How much time do we have?" I pull my knees to my chest and wrap my arms around them.

"The three of you are connecting strongly with Spirit. Leo is, too, but he won't accept it yet. This connection will help you to counteract the evil that is growing." Zeke rips up a clump of grass and lets it flutter to the ground through his fingers.

"Lorraine and I don't know the future, only possibilities. As events occur on Earth, those possibilities change. The changes are like a child's kaleidoscope. When you move it slightly, the glass pieces shift and the picture you see changes. The Native shamans and Ascended Masters are monitoring events on Earth very closely. But it's sometimes frustrating for us not to know whether our efforts will be successful or if there will be enough time."

He leans forward. "What we are doing together does matter, though. You will take what you learn and share it with others. At a certain point, a critical level of positive vibrational energy will be achieved to tip the balance for Earth, and she will move to the Fifth Dimension."

He opens his hands, palms up toward the sky. "We just don't know when that will be."

"Or if it will be in time," I reply. A chill runs down my spine.

"Yes," he says simply.

"If it's important to raise the vibrational energy of people to reach that critical point, then why don't we focus on humans instead of Earth in the meditation?" Eric asks.

"That's a very good question." Lorraine tells him. She's returned to a sitting position. "The meditation focus on Earth does help in raising human consciousness, but we've also planned meditations to connect with others, to influence the consciousness of all of humanity."

"So what does it mean exactly to ascend to the Fifth Dimension?" I ask.

"It is the next step in the evolutionary process of humankind. Cro-Magnon man had to evolve in intelligence to survive. This human evolution is the elevation of consciousness," she says. "If it doesn't happen, humankind will eventually cause its own destruction and that of Earth."

I sit down next to Leo on one of the benches surrounding the bonfire. It's getting late, but there are still a few people gathered around the dying embers. He's sitting by himself, a little apart from the others, staring at the fire, which is good because I want to talk to him alone. Leo glances up at me when I sit down, and his smile lights up his face and eyes. I release the breath I'd been holding. I wasn't sure what my reception would be.

"Hey," I say.

"Hey." He reaches for my hand.

"Soooo, you left kind of abruptly," I tell him. I see no point in beating around the bush; might as well get it out in the open right away.

"Yeah, about that." He runs his other hand through his hair and rubs the back of his neck. "It's not you. You know that, right?"

"I know. I understand that this stuff's hard to believe—hard to accept. I get that. I just want to share it with you."

"I'd like that, too, but I'm not where you are with it. This whole thing with the Zeke and Lorraine and the Fifth Dimension and Earth ascending is all so completely the opposite of everything I've ever thought to be true. I'm just not sure I buy into it. I'm kind of a see-it-to-believe-it guy."

"But you did see it!" My voice rises even though I'm trying to be quiet. "You saw Zeke raise the stone, and you had the vision on Greystone Mountain, and then tonight's meditation . . ."

"I don't know." He sighs. "I'm pretty sure I didn't see what you did in the meditation." He bumps his elbow into my side. "I didn't see any blue light. And thankfully, I didn't feel anything negative, either. Maybe I saw the Earth's aura and the ley lines. But what if all of it is just my imagination?"

"It wasn't your imagination," I say in what I hope is an understanding voice, even though I'm frustrated. "Those things are real. I know it." I move our clasped hands from my knee to my lap and grasp his hand in both of mine. "Will you just promise me that you'll try to be open to it and keep showing up? I think it's important."

"Well, I'm flattered you think it's important I'm there, although I'm not sure that's true. If it means spending more time with you, then I think I can promise that." He's very close now and leaning toward me so our faces are only inches apart.

"Good," I breathe out right before he kisses me.

14

ERIC AND DREW are waiting for me by the shelter when I open the farmhouse door on Sunday morning, which is a surprise. I forgot Drew spent the night in Eric's room; also, it's usually me who's waiting for Eric.

"I'm going to take Drew over to Mom and Dad at the staff dorm before we go running. They'll probably be making something for breakfast," he says.

"Yeah, like bacon," Drew says happily.

Eric ruffles his hair. "Knowing how much you like bacon, I'm sure they're making some just for you."

"OK. I'll catch up with you in a few."

Renee, Lainey, and Nora are sleeping in. I didn't want to wake them and everyone else by clomping on the creaky old wooden floor and stairs this early in the morning, so I carried my shoes. I sit down on the nearest bench to slip the shoes on. A big storm came through during the night with thunder and lightning and heavy rain. There are a few puddles here and there in the clearing, but the early morning air is clear and fresh, and the sun is shining. Perfect weather for a run.

Breakfast is well underway when I arrive at the staff dorm to meet Eric. No one is trying to be quiet here. My dad's frying up bacon, as expected, and my mom is making blueberry pancakes. Dr. Fraser and Zeke and another graduate student are seated at the table with their coffees and plates of partially demolished pancakes. Eric and Drew are already at the stove filling up their own plates. Everyone is talking.

"Good morning, sunshine!" my dad calls out to me. "Would you like some breakfast?"

"I'd love some, but I don't think I can eat a full breakfast before we go running. Maybe I'll just snag a few bites from Drew." I pluck a fork off the counter and hold it poised over his plate. I give him my sweetest big sister smile.

"Okaaayyy," Drew says.

I take a bite of pancake smothered in real maple syrup and the hot blueberries explode in my mouth.

"Hi, honey." My mom puts her arm around my shoulders and gives me a squeeze. "Did you sleep well, with the storms last night?" She knows I like thunderstorms.

"Yes, I slept great. Thanks for breakfast. The pancakes are delicious. Save me some?" I snag a piece of bacon.

"Sure. Why don't you make up a plate? I'll set it aside. You can heat it up when you get back."

"Good idea." I put three pancakes and three more pieces of bacon on a plate and hand it to Mom.

She covers it and puts it toward the back of the counter. Since Eric has no qualms about running on a full stomach, I sit down at the end of the table to wait while he eats. I nod hello to Zeke and Dr. Fraser.

"I thought we could run along the road that goes past Pops and Nana's farmhouse," Eric says to me from across the table.

"I drove the route the other day. It's about six miles. Can you do that?"

I decide not to get ticked about this question because he's asking in a friendly—not competitive—way. "Sure, we run that much every day in cross-country practice."

Eric has to run a lot for soccer, but the motto of cross-country is "our sport is your sport's punishment," so even though he's a guy and taller than me, we're pretty even in our running ability. I also run the mid distances in track. I'm not sure which of us would win in a sprint.

"Please be careful running on those country roads," my mom says. "People drive really fast and might not see you."

"We will. Don't worry." Eric takes a gulp of orange juice and looks toward me. "Are you ready?"

"Almost. I want to stretch a bit first." Outside on the porch, I lean against one of the posts and stretch out my calves and hamstrings, then pull my feet back one at a time to stretch my quads.

Eric comes out after me and lets the door slam behind him. I wonder if the other graduate students are trying to sleep in spite of the racket taking place downstairs.

"Ready," I say.

We start off with a slow jog along the main road of the Angel Mounds site. No cars are parked in front of the visitor center, as it's too early for it to be open. There aren't many cars on the main road, and we run side by side against traffic so we can see oncoming cars. The corn on either side of the road is a little over knee high. The only sound besides our breathing and the slap of our feet on the road is the hum of insects in the fields.

I love the rhythm of running and the power and strength I feel in my body when I run. There's a certain zen aspect to it, almost like a meditation, when you really get in the flow of movement. You can turn off your mind and let your body take over.

We run for a few minutes in silence, settling into our pace. "What do you think about Zeke and Lorraine, and about what they're telling us?" Eric interjects into the quiet. "You seem to be pretty much on board with it."

I figured this was one of the reasons Eric suggested we go for a run together, so we could talk about what's going on. I'm glad to have someone besides Leo and Renee to talk with.

"Aren't you? It's a lot like the stuff you study in Dr. Auberge's lab, isn't it?" I say between breaths. The pace we're running isn't too strenuous, so talking is still possible.

"Some of it is, yeah. I guess the part I'm not sure about is that there's something I have to do, that I actually *can* do, to stop Earth's destruction. It sounds a little crazy even saying it. I mean, it's such a monumental task. Who am I for it to be me?"

"I know what you mean. As much as I buy into what they're saying about fear and evil taking over the planet, it's kind of scary to think about going up against it. Would those forces retaliate against us personally . . . like the jerks at the coffee shop?" I don't tell him about how, when I connect with Zeke and Lorraine, it feels as though I'm opening like the petals of a flower, unfurling to face the sun. I almost feel like a puzzle piece that was missing has slipped into place. Zeke and Lorraine have brought me what I've been yearning for. But it comes with a price.

Our feet pound out a constant beat on the gravelly shoulder of the road. A cloud of midges surrounds our heads, and I close my mouth to avoid swallowing one. We both swat at them to clear the air, but still they follow us for a while before moving off.

When we can open our mouths again, Eric says, "You saw how Renee reacted last night."

I nod and realize that he isn't looking at me. "Yeah."

"She's sort of pissed at me for being able to connect more than her. And at you too."

"Really? That doesn't seem like her."

"Maybe that's the wrong word. She's frustrated and afraid. I think being pissed at me distracts her from those other thoughts. When Zeke told her it was her own fear that was attracting the negative energy, she really went off."

"I think it's true, though, don't you?"

"In a way, I do, which makes it harder. I want to be sympathetic, but I also want to be working on connecting more myself and not spending so much time calming her down. Zeke says it's part of my role to show her the way. I'm trying to be supportive, but it gets old." He spits onto the road.

Gross. Why do guys do that?

"I have a strong feeling that Leo is supposed to be involved, but he's really resistant."

"So, you and Leo, huh?" Eric says.

A blush creeps up my neck and cheeks. "Hmmm, yeah." Maybe we're old enough now that he won't tease me.

"He seems like a good guy," is all he replies.

We turn onto the road where the farmhouse is located. The sun has risen higher into the sky. I'm glad I remembered to put on sunscreen and wear a baseball cap.

"Want to pick up the pace a bit?" Eric asks.

"Sure," I say, and we speed up.

I drop back behind Eric as a car comes toward us, so he sees the farmhouse before I do.

"Shit!" he yells.

"What is it? Did you twist your ankle?" That's the first thought that pops into my head, but he's running fine. In fact, he's sprinting toward the house.

I catch up to him, then I see it too. A scarecrow is stuck into the middle of the front yard, smoking and smoldering. It's a charred and blackened effigy, and it gives me a sick feeling in the pit of my stomach. An acrid burning smell reaches my nostrils. As we get closer to the house, we can see that whoever left the scarecrow also left a message in the grass. *GO HOME* is burned in large block letters across the front yard. I haven't been exposed to much evil in my life, but that's exactly how this feels—evil. Someone hates us. And wants to harm us.

A white pickup truck is still in the driveway. The engine starts as we come running up. The windows are rolled up and tinted, so we can't see inside.

Eric yells, "Hey!" and sprints toward the truck, but it accelerates quickly onto the road, sending gravel flying. He runs after it for a few yards but soon realizes there's nothing he can do and stops. He walks slowly back to where I'm standing in front of the house, still dazed.

Whoever did this also threw clumps of dirt, or maybe something worse, onto the white clapboards of the front porch. The whole thing leaves me feeling personally and physically violated.

"Did you see the license plate? I didn't catch it," Eric's breathing heavily from the sprint and stands with his hands on his hips.

"No, I'm sorry. I wasn't really thinking clearly enough for that. I can't believe someone would do this." My legs feel wobbly and I lower myself to the grass before I fall.

Eric indicates the words burned into the grass. "That's what the guy at the coffee shop said to me. 'Go home.' Bastard."

"Do you think it's the same guy?" I clench my hands in my lap to stop them from shaking.

"I don't know." He wipes his face with his shirt. "What if they'd burned the damn house down?" he says with controlled fury, kicking at a clump of grass.

"They wouldn't do something like that," I say, appalled.

"Scott said some pretty nasty stuff happened in Kansas."

We look in stunned silence for a few minutes at the evidence of hatred. Finally I say, "I think we need to call Dad." I pull out my cell phone. "And the police."

Dad pulls up in his old Audi about ten minutes later. His car was old five years ago, but he says it runs fine and he doesn't need a new car, just a reliable one. He shuts off the engine halfway up the driveway and steps out. Dr. Fraser and Zeke are with him.

"You two OK?" he asks us.

We're sitting under the huge maple tree, leaning against its trunk. It seems like a long time ago that we were here for the fracking meeting, but it was only yesterday morning.

"I'm OK. Just a little wobbly." I'm trying to hide it, but I'm shaken up by the vandalism. "It's hard to believe someone would do this. That someone hates us this much."

Dad squats down and wraps his arms around my shoulders. I unsuccessfully try to stifle a sob.

"It's OK, honey." He pats my back. "I'm sorry this happened. And sorry, too, Eric, about what happened in town yesterday. I feel responsible." He rubs his hand across his forehead. "If we hadn't had the meeting yesterday, this wouldn't have happened."

"It's not your fault." I lean back from him. "You're not responsible for how other people behave. We know how destructive and toxic fracking is. We're right to stand up to the big energy companies. They have no qualms about poisoning our water."

He pats my arm, and I put my hand on his. "I'm proud that you're the person who stands up," I tell him. "Whatever happens."

"Thank you," he says. "I just don't want to put you kids or your mother in any danger."

Dr. Fraser is looking down at the letters burned into the grass. "It looks like they used gasoline to burn the letters. Somewhat incongruous," he says.

Eric rolls his eyes. "So far they've really only threatened us, not actually harmed us."

"They punched you in the face!" I exclaim. His hand moves to touch his eye.

"I haven't forgotten. Every step on the run is jarring."

"It's very important to stand up for what's right, and it takes courage. I commend you. We may all need that courage in the time to come," Zeke says.

"I hope this will be the end of it." My dad glances over to the driveway as a blue and white police cruiser pulls in.

"I wish I *had* punched the guy in the coffee shop. At least then I'd feel like I'd done something, instead of feeling frustrated and powerless," Eric seems more pissed than upset. It's probably a defense against feeling victimized, but at least it's working.

"These are my children, Eric and Marcie," my dad tells the officer. "They found the scarecrow when they were out running."

The officer turns to us. "Tell me what happened." She's small and slight, hardly over five feet tall, with close-cropped dark hair. Eric tells her about our run, seeing the scarecrow and the message, and about the white pickup driving away. She writes everything down in a notebook.

"I'm sorry we didn't get the license plate number," I add, feeling like I've let her down somehow.

Dr. Fraser joins us then. He'd been over by the porch inspecting the crap flung on the walls.

"From the look and smell of the stuff, I think it's probably horse or cow manure." He rocks back on his heels, somewhat pleased to be offering this information.

Crap indeed.

"Thank you. It's not hard to come by around here," the officer says, deadpan.

"Yes, I suppose you're right," Dr. Fraser replies, not abashed in the slightest.

"You should also know that Eric was involved in a bit of a confrontation in the coffee shop in town yesterday," my dad tells the officer.

She looks at Eric, and he blushes self-consciously. He relays what happened.

"Do you think this could be related?" she asks, her pen poised over her notebook.

"It may or may not be the same person, but they're definitely related," my dad says. "We held an antifracking informational meeting here yesterday morning. The message here is pretty clear, and the young man who punched Eric took offense to what he sees as our meddling in local affairs."

"After he punched me he told me to 'go home,'" Eric says. "There were a lot of witnesses. The owner of the coffee shop apologized to me and made him and his friends leave. She called him Robby."

"Did you press charges?" she asks.

"No, we didn't." My dad sighs and rubs his hand over his face. "I don't know if we want to go that route, given the antagonism some people are already feeling. However, a visit from the police certainly wouldn't hurt."

"I'd like to take some pictures of your injuries to have on file in the event that you do decide to prosecute at some point in the future," she tells Eric as she pulls out a small camera.

"Sure. It's just the black eye." Eric stands still while she snaps a few shots of his face and a close-up of his eye.

"I'll file a report about this incident and see what kind of vehicles this Robby and his friends drive. I'll definitely be paying them a visit and will let you know what we find out. Call me if anything else occurs." She flips her notebook closed and hands my dad a card. "Here's my number."

After she leaves, Eric and I find a hose and some rags and a bucket in the garage. I hook the hose up to the faucet. We sluice the manure off the porch and wipe off the residue that remains. A few spots on the porch are stained a faint greenish color. Maybe they will fade away eventually, or maybe the stains will remain as a reminder. I find myself wanting them to stay visible.

"You guys OK?" Zeke joins us.

"I guess." I wring out my rag. "It doesn't feel very good to be the target of something like this. We're just one family against a huge corporation. Can we really make a difference?"

"In the coming months and years, as the duality between fear and love increases, there'll be more things like this happening," he says.

I look at him with some alarm.

"Not necessarily to you personally," he says quickly, "but around the world. When the forces of light and love rise up, the forces of fear and hate will push back."

"What are we supposed to do about it?" The feeling of powerlessness returns.

"You're already doing it. Just being present and raising your spiritual consciousness and connecting with other Light Workers is enormously important. I know it may not appear that way now, but you have to trust it's true and that you're making a difference and you will continue to make a difference." He takes a rag from the bucket and scrubs at a spot on the porch. "You're only seeing the negativity that resulted from yesterday's meeting. Many people left the meeting with a new understanding of their responsibility to Earth. Many souls are awakening to the message."

"If you say so. But I'm still pissed about this," Eric says.

Zeke throws his head back and laughs. Not the reaction I was expecting.

"If your anger helps you stay focused and motivated, then use it," he says with a smile. "Just don't let it take over and turn into something more." He places a hand on Eric's shoulder. "I don't think that will be a problem for you. You have a good heart."

"Thank you," Eric says, awkwardly.

"You're welcome. May I?" He reaches his hand toward Eric's face.

"OK."

Zeke places his palm over Eric's eye, the golden light emanating from his hand. I look over my shoulder to where my dad and Dr. Fraser are standing, but they're not paying any attention to us.

"How's that?" Zeke removes his hand.

"Better." Eric gingerly touches the area around his eye.

"The swelling and pain will clear up in a couple of hours. Here, I'll help you put these things away." We gather up the bucket and hose and return them to the garage.

I feel a lot better than I did earlier, but not completely back to normal. I need to expend the pent-up negative energy that's still coursing through me. A run is just what I need.

"Do you want to finish our run?" I ask Eric.

"Yeah, definitely."

"Want company?" Zeke asks us.

Dad and Dr. Fraser have finished disposing of the charred scarecrow and are already in the car. I look pointedly down at Zeke's hiking sandals. He sees my glance and says, "I've had to run in them before." I wonder, not for the first time, what Zeke and Lorraine were doing before coming to the dig.

"Nah, that's OK," Eric says. "We'll be fine. The worst is over."

We wait a few minutes for the cloud of exhaust from the Audi to dissipate before starting the return run. We don't talk, and at first our pace is easy and slow, but after the first mile, by unspoken agreement, we really kick it into high gear, going almost full out.

I'm sprinting like I'm trying to catch something or like something's chasing me. Maybe there is. All I know is that by the time I arrive back at the clearing, my shirt plastered to my back with sweat and my chest heaving, I've left it behind.

15

THE NATIVE AMERICAN spirits have been communicating with me all morning. In fact, they communicate with me whenever I'm on the dig site. We're pretty sure the area Leo, Scott, and I are working on used to be a dwelling of some sort. Scott and I have uncovered portions of a wall, and Leo is working on an area that was a firepit.

I have a strong sense of the family who lived here, seeing glimpses of them going about their daily activities, making tools and preparing food. In my mind's eye I see a woman grinding corn in a shallow wooden bowl with a stone tool. A man, presumably her husband or partner, is shaping pieces of stone into knife points and arrowheads. The section I'm working on appears to be the tool-making area of the dwelling. I've found flakes of chert left over from his flint knapping, a method of creating a tool by skillfully knocking off pieces of the stone to create a sharp edge. I've also found a knife blade and several arrowheads. It's pretty freaking amazing to see him flint knapping in my mind and then find the tangible evidence of what he was doing.

I'm so immersed in the scene I even feel the affection the man and woman have for one another. I've accepted that these visions aren't just my imagination. Just like with the Native girl from my summer at the lake, I'm actually seeing these people from hundreds of years ago. This time, though, they aren't interacting with me directly like she did, they're simply showing me what their lives were like. At first I felt a little like a voyeur, but I've come to appreciate the visions as a gift.

No remnants of the actual building material of the wall remain, though. It decomposed long ago, and what I see instead is a darker area of dirt where the organic material of the wooden posts left traces behind. The wall runs straight for several meters, with posts roughly every fifty centimeters, to a corner where it turns. It looks like the wall will continue on to the area Scott's uncovered. We're spaced about ten meters from each other and are working so we'll meet and join the two sections of wall.

It's been overcast and threatening rain all morning, but so far the forecasted storms have held off. I'm glad; I find excavation really absorbing. It's fascinating to watch the past unfold before my eyes as I remove layers of dirt with my trowel and uncover artifacts and physical features.

I'm completely engrossed in what I'm doing, transported back to the time of the Native Americans who lived here, connecting with their spirits, when Leo plops down beside me, startling me so much that I jump and let out a little yelp.

"Sorry," he says. "I didn't mean to scare you. You're pretty focused on what you're doing." He does that thing where he nudges me in the side with his elbow. "You really like this work."

I smile, a little embarrassed. "I do like it. I feel like I'm on a treasure hunt." I set my trowel down and lean back on my hands. "What about you? Do you think this is what you'd like to do as your career?"

I decided after the meditation Saturday night not to press Leo about his opinions on fracking or his feelings toward Zeke and Lorraine. I think it would do more harm than good if I try to force it, anyway.

"Something like this. I'm hoping to get a chance to talk to your mom and Dr. Fraser about what it's like." Leo's Mediterranean skin is a dusky tan from spending so much time in the sun. It's only a few shades lighter than his hair and eyes, and his teeth gleam whitely in the midst of all his shades of brown. Of course it makes him even more beautiful. Can you call a boy beautiful?

Our knees are touching, and the contrast between my pale knee and his brown one is striking. I realize I've fallen hard for Leo.

"My mom would love to talk with you. She says part of what she likes about being a professor is helping her students decide what career path they want to take." I reach for my water bottle to mask my sudden nervousness after my realization. I unscrew the top before taking a long drink, then wipe my face with my bandana.

The air is heavy with humidity. Even though the sun isn't out, it's still very warm, but that's not why I'm perspiring.

"Hey, I found something. A piece of pottery, I think," Scott calls out.

Leo and I crawl over to see what he's uncovered. It's not like we could get any dirtier than we already are, and I'm still wearing my gloves. For a few minutes we watch him carefully remove dirt from around a large shard of pottery. It emerges, appearing to be a portion of a bowl with a scalloped rim. He continues to work, and we go back to our own sections.

It's a little too early to take a full break, but I decide to switch from excavating to diagramming the wall and the artifacts I found onto my graph paper. I can look over the top of my clipboard and watch Leo work while I draw. He has his back to me and is bent over his section. His hair falls in waves down his neck, and the muscles of his back and arms bunch and stretch as he moves. I reluctantly pull my attention back to my graph and plot the distance of each portion of the wall in relation to the data point in my section. The data points were fixed for all the one-by-one-meter sections when Zeke, Lorraine, and the other graduate students conducted the survey and mapped out the whole site.

Scott uncovers several pottery shards, enough to make up almost a complete bowl. It's exciting to find a nearly complete artifact, and he's clearly pleased about it.

"Are you going to show Dr. Fraser and catalog the bowl?" I ask him.

Since we're destroying the site as we excavate, we have to meticulously catalog the placement of each item we find. The diagrams we make of our discoveries on our individual worksheets are next transferred onto the master diagram of the site that my mom keeps. We also take a lot of pictures and samples of the dirt from the features we uncover and take copious notes about our findings.

"Yeah, I'm going over there right now." He places the shards in an artifact bag and stands up.

"I'll go with you. I have a few things to catalogue." I take my artifact bags containing the knife and arrowheads and follow Scott.

We log our artifacts into the catalogue book that hangs on a hook inside the trailer and label our bags before placing them in the storage boxes. They'll be cleaned and analyzed back in the labs at the university along with the rest of the items we collect from the field study.

When I get back to my section, I position myself with my back to Leo so I won't be tempted to look at him and get distracted.

As lunchtime approaches, I've started feeling more sympathetic toward Leo. I understand that maybe his reluctance is as much because of fear as anything else. I know I'm supposed to help him, but I don't really know what I can do that will help. I wrap up before he and Scott finish and find Lainey so we can eat together. Renee joins us on the picnic bench. It's nice to just have some girl talk for a change and not think about the vandalism at the farm, or fracking, or the Fifth Dimension.

Lainey has a crush on Scott, and Renee and I are encouraging her to make some sort of move. "The field study is only six weeks long," Renee says. "You don't want to waste the time you could be spending with him on working up the courage to let him know. Try flirting with him and see how he responds."

"I'm pretty sure he was checking you out when we were in town," I say. "Anyway, you're the whole package, pretty, curvy in all the right places, smart, fun. What's not to like?"

"What've you got to lose?" Renee says between bites.

"My pride?" Lainey laughs. I can see why Scott would be interested in her. Her dimpled smile is infectious.

"If he's not interested, which we already know he is, then you've lost nothing. But if he is, then you've got five weeks of fun with Scott!" Renee tells her.

All this talk of how much time is left in the field study makes me think about Leo and me. The university he attends is in the town where I live, but what will happen when I go back to high school and he goes back to college? Will he still want to date a high school girl?

Back at the dig, I return easily to the rhythm of excavating. At some point the Native spirits return, their thoughts mingling with mine, guiding me, and I find myself moving to another section of the dwelling, adjacent to where I'd been working. There's something they want me to find. I feel no sense of urgency, just a gentle prodding, almost like an intuition, telling me that what I'm looking for is here. I'm drawn to a corner of the new section and carefully remove layers of dirt with my trowel. It takes me almost forty-five minutes, but I'm enfolded in a trancelike state, not in any hurry. Then my trowel strikes something hard, and I become fully aware.

Carefully, I remove dirt from around the object, and its shape emerges. It's long and cylindrical, about two inches in diameter and eight inches long, with faceted sides. It looks like a tool of some sort. When the last bit of dirt encasing it in the ground falls away, I see that it's a large, pale pink crystal.

I take off my gloves to pick it up and turn it over in my hands. A powerful frisson of energy emanates from the crystal, giving me the sensation of a mild electric jolt. I sense a faintly audible humming sound or vibration in the air. The crystal's sides are hard and smooth like glass; the ends form pointed triangular pyramids. My fingers feel indentations on one side. I reach into my toolbox for a bandana and gently rub the indented area to remove the embedded dirt. There's a symbol of some sort carved into the side of the crystal. I brush the worst of the dirt off, and the facets glint in the faint light of the overcast day.

Renee is working on a section of the site that was used as a refuse area. I want to show the crystal to her first. Whatever it is, I know it's something very important. I can feel its energy and know the Native spirits showed me where to find it.

I kneel beside her. "Look what I found." I hold the crystal in my palms and let it roll so she can see the carving.

It's a circle with a triangle superimposed over it. The crystal sparkles faintly.

"That was in your section?" She rocks back on her heels and peers down at it. "I think it's rose quartz." She reaches out her index finger to touch the carving. Her eyes widen, and I know she can sense the energy contained in the crystal. "I wonder what this symbol means?"

"I was guided to find it. I think it's important somehow."

"Maybe we should show it to Lorraine," Renee says.

Lorraine is seated under the open-sided tent that serves as a work area. She's transferring information onto the main map of the site. Her head is bent over the table, her braid draped over one shoulder, hanging into her lap. She looks up from the graph as we approach, brushing strands of hair from her face where it's curled in the humid air.

"I found this in my section. Renee thinks it's a rose quartz crystal." I hand it to her. "The Native spirits showed me where to find it."

When I place the crystal in her hand, it sparkles more brightly.

"It's exquisite," she says. "You're right. It's a rose quartz." She turns the crystal over. When she sees the symbol, she breathes in deeply and brushes her fingers over it reverentially. "This is the Sacred Triangle, the symbol of the partnership between the Native peoples, the Ascended Masters, and the Light Workers for the protection and ascension of Earth." She raises her eyes to meet mine. "The Native spirits have guided you to a powerful tool for the Ascension, Marcie. Crystals are used as activators and record keepers. Pink is the color of the heart chakra. The Sacred Triangle amplifies the capabilities already imbedded in the crystal."

TRACY RICHARDSON

"What capabilities? What are we supposed to do with it?" I ask, eager to finally be doing something to help instead of waiting and learning.

"It was shown to you for a reason, but you will have to discover for yourself what that purpose is."

This deflates my eagerness like a punctured balloon. "Why can't you just tell us what we're supposed to do and be done with it? Why does the information have to be doled out in bits and pieces?" Tears of anger and frustration well up in my eyes; I quickly swipe them away.

Lorraine gives me an understanding look, which just adds to my annoyance. "This is *your* journey," she says. "You must go through the steps in order to learn and grow. As with all of life, it's a process." She hands the crystal back to me, and a tingling sensation radiates up my arm when I grasp it.

"Really, that's it? That's the 'guidance' you're giving me? Find my own way?" The words pour out of me. "I can't believe you say you're here to help us and then you hand the crystal back to me and tell me to figure it out myself." I have a childish desire to vent my anger by flinging the crystal and smashing it against the side of the trailer, but I fling my angry thoughts toward Lorraine instead.

She recoils slightly as though she's received a physical blow from the assault of my thoughts. A flicker of pain crosses her normally serene features. "I'm sorry, Marcie. You all have a very important task here on Earth. Please know we are helping in every way we can, but we cannot do everything for you." The ache of her desire to help comes to me in waves across the short distance between us, causing my anger to fizzle out.

Her response to my outburst is compassion and love. How can I ascend to the Fifth Dimension when I can't control myself and lash out at someone who's trying to help me?

124

"Also," Lorraine continues, "I'm not omniscient. I have a sense of things to come, but I can't predict the future. It is yours to choose."

I'm not sure if that makes me feel better or worse, and I still don't know what to do with the crystal. I stay silent while I try to quell my churning emotions.

"What does the circle in the symbol represent?" Renee asks, breaking the tension and allowing me time to regroup.

"The circle is the symbol for Earth. She's protected by the three sides of the triangle, each representing one of the elements of the partnership." Lorraine flips her braid over her shoulder and gestures to two camp chairs. "Why don't you two sit down?"

We pull the chairs over beside her. I sink into one, grateful to not have to contribute for the moment.

"Who are the Ascended Masters?" Renee asks. This is the most engaged with Lorraine that I've seen her. There's no trace of fear.

"They are spiritual masters who ascended to the Fifth Dimension. They have achieved a high level of consciousness and serve to guide Light Workers here on Earth. You know some of them: Buddha; Jesus, or Sananda as he is known to us; Rumi, the Sufi poet and mystic; Mohammad; Moses; Quan Yin, the bodhisattva of compassion; and others who are not known to you. They are working to guide and protect Earth and humans during this critical period while Earth transitions into the new age of enlightenment."

She crosses her legs and leans back in her chair. "The Mayan calendar that ended on December 21, 2012, did not predict the end of time on Earth but the beginning of a new era. Earth is now in alignment with the Central Sun of the galaxy and will soon be connecting with the Fifth Dimension. It's an extremely important event."

I've finally regained my composure and I feel terrible for my outburst. "I'm sorry I got upset with you," I tell Lorraine. "Patience isn't one of my strengths." I shrug sheepishly. "Or kindness. Or gratitude. There's probably a long list of things I can improve on. Thank you for what you and Zeke are doing to help all of us on Earth. I shouldn't repay you by biting your head off."

"No need to apologize to me for what is really one of your strengths. You are a person of action, and that is something to be celebrated and proud of."

"Thank you."

"You're willing to take new challenges head on." She pulls gently on my ponytail. "I know you have a kind heart. You'll learn patience as well."

"Oh no, not another learning experience," I say. I can't help it. It's so true.

Renee and I get up to leave, and Lorraine stands as well.

"You are both doing exceptional work." She places a hand on each of our shoulders. Her touch has a calming effect, replacing my tumultuous emotions. "Never doubt that you are on the right track."

"I'm not sure if I should keep the crystal or put it in with the other artifacts," I say to Renee as we leave the tent, the crystal a warm weight in my palm. "What do you think?"

She furrows her brow, considering, then reaches out to take the crystal from me. "It seems like—until we know more—the safest place to put it is with the other artifacts. We'll know where it is if we need to get it."

She walks with me to the trailer where I place the crystal in an artifact bag and log it in. I decide to call it a "digging tool." I

126

don't want to draw undue attention to it. I jot down its number and location on a scrap of paper so I can retrieve it later.

"I know you want all the answers right away," Renee says as we return to our sections, "but I'm actually glad they aren't dumping everything on us all at once. I'm having trouble assimilating the information as it is."

I know she's right. I suddenly feel exhausted from the roller coaster of emotions I've been through today. It's almost four o'clock, which is when we usually wrap up for the day, so I decide to just pack it in now and maybe go take a nap. I've had enough excitement for today.

16

Wednesday night I'm on dinner duty. I volunteered to do setup and cleanup, so I won't be needed for the predinner prep. This gives me time for a quick run after we finish at the site for the day. Eric got roped into cooking the meal, which is hilarious since he's never cooked anything that required more action than sliding a pizza in the oven or melting a cheese quesadilla in the toaster oven.

I've run past Pops and Nana's house the last two days, for my own peace of mind, but haven't seen any signs of more vandalism. This afternoon I take the opposite direction toward the boat launch area on the river. The launch is about the halfway point of my run, so I stop to sit on the rocky embankment next to the ramp for a few minutes, where I can watch the green-brown water flow slowly past. It's a good place to gather my thoughts.

Excitement and fear wage a war inside my head. I want to be part of what's happening with Zeke and Lorraine, but I'm not entirely sure what is actually happening or what my part in it is supposed to be. I try not to dwell on it for too long, though. Better not to analyze it too deeply, or I might totally freak out.

When I get back to the camp area, I have just enough time to take a quick shower before joining Scott and Leo to set out plates, silverware, and drinks for dinner in the shelter. Lainey, Renee, and Eric made spaghetti and meatballs to be accompanied by salad and garlic bread. As I'm carrying out one of the huge bowls of spaghetti from the dorm kitchen to the shelter, I hear tires crunching on the gravel of the parking area.

A white van with the red and blue United Energy logo is pulling into a parking spot. I stop walking so abruptly that the spaghetti sloshes in the bowl, splashing tomato sauce over the rim onto the grass, narrowly missing my feet. As I watch, the silver-haired man from the meeting on Saturday and a man wearing suit pants and a starched button-down shirt get out. I quickly sidestep the tomato sauce, set the bowl down on the serving table, and walk over to see what the hell these guys want, mentally preparing myself for a confrontation.

The man in the starched shirt steps forward as I approach like he's in charge. He puts on a big smile and extends his hand to me.

"Hello, I'm James Stamatakis. You may know my son, Leo? He's on the dig here this summer. I thought I'd surprise him with a visit while I was in Evansville for a meeting. Do you happen to know where he might be?"

Leo's dad.

"Sure. He's around here somewhere. I'll go get him." I glance over at the United Energy guy, not bothering to hide my hostility.

Mr. Stamatakis sees my look. "Stuart offered to give me a ride out here after I finished my meetings with United Energy this afternoon," he says in an affable voice. I can tell he's got to know about our antifracking meeting on Saturday. Something is going on here, but I'm not sure what it is. I'm about to turn to go find Leo when he appears beside me.

"Dad! What are you doing here?" He's slightly out of breath like he ran over.

"I had some meetings with United Energy in Evansville, and I thought I'd drop by to see you. I want to check out what you're doing on the field study and meet your friends and professors." He takes a step toward Leo and puts his hand on his shoulder. "It's good to see you, son. Why don't you show me around and introduce me?"

"You could have told me you were coming. I'm on dinner duty tonight. I'm supposed to be setting up." He looks at me apologetically.

"Don't worry about it. We're almost done and ready to eat anyway," I say. The good manners my parents have drilled into me kick in, and I invite them to stay for dinner.

"Thank you, I think we'll take you up on that offer. What's your name?"

So far the United Energy guy hasn't said a word, which is surprising given how confidently he spoke at the meeting. I guess this is Mr. Stamatakis's show.

"Marcie Horton," I say. "My mom's the lead archaeologist on the dig," I add, mostly for the benefit of the United Energy guy, in case he knows about my family from the antifracking meeting.

I leave them so I can finish bringing out the rest of the food. Scott is on his way out with the salad when I get there.

"Hey, hold up a minute." I put my hand on Scott's arm to get his attention, and we step to the side of the path to allow others to pass by. "Leo's dad just showed up, and he brought the guy from United Energy. Leo's dad said he had a meeting with the guys from United Energy today."

"No shit? What's that all about?" He adjusts his grip on the bowl of salad, balancing it on his hip.

"I'm pretty sure Leo told us at one point that his dad works for the Department of Energy. It may be nothing, but it's hard to believe this timing is a coincidence. I just wanted you to know. I'll try to sit by them at dinner."

"OK. I'll see if I can too." Scott continues on toward the shelter to deposit the salad, and I head inside to see if there's anything left to bring out.

When all the food and plates are set out, we ring the big dinner bell outside the girls' farmhouse. I hang back to see where Leo and his dad will sit. People emerge from the dorms and arrive from where they were hanging out outside. Everyone lines up by the serving tables. My mom and Dr. Fraser and the graduate students are walking in small groups down the path that leads to the staff dorm. Leo and the two cronies, as I've started thinking of them, are waiting at the end of the path for the others. I walk over quickly. When I get there, Leo is making introductions.

"It's nice to meet you, Mr. Stamatakis." My mom shakes his hand.

"Call me James. Thank you for giving Leo such a wonderful experience. He's really enjoying himself. You're doing excellent work here." He gestures to the silver-haired man. "I think you may already know Stuart Houseman."

My mom's eyes widen when she recognizes the United Energy guy, but she retains her composure. She shakes his hand and says pointedly, "Yes, I remember you from our antifracking meeting last Saturday."

There's a heightened tension in the air which increases when Zeke steps forward to introduce himself. "I'm Zeke Waterson, Leo's graduate student advisor on the dig, and this is Lorraine Tressler, his other advisor." Zeke indicates Lorraine, who steps up beside him.

This is the first time I've ever heard their last names. On some level I must have known they had last names, but I've also been thinking of them as just appearing out of nowhere to be at the dig.

An irrational fear that everyone there can see Zeke and Lorraine for who and what they are briefly overcomes me, but it quickly passes. They do have an undeniable presence about them. But then Mr. Stamatakis inhales sharply at Zeke's appearance, and a niggling uneasiness curls in my stomach. What does he know about Zeke and Lorraine? Why is he here, exactly?

"Good to meet the two of you." Mr. Stamatakis shakes both of their hands. "Leo's been telling me all about you. Why don't we sit together at dinner? I want to hear about your experiences on the digs you've been on."

What has Leo been telling him?

I follow the group through the food line, then take a seat next to Leo and his dad. I nod at Scott when he sits down next to Zeke, opposite me.

"What's your background?" Mr. Stamatakis asks Zeke.

"Lorraine and I are graduate students at the university studying archaeology. Our focus is the Native cultures of the Americas." Zeke dips his garlic bread into the tomato sauce on his plate and takes a bite.

"Before that we studied at Washington State University," Lorraine adds.

"So are you two a couple?" Mr. Stamatakis points to them both in turn with his fork.

I'm kind of pissed on their behalf that he would ask such a personal question, even though I've wondered the same thing myself and didn't have the nerve to ask.

Lorraine lays her hand on Zeke's arm. "Yes, we're partners."

Zeke covers her hand with his in what feels like an intimate gesture. I feel stupid for not realizing before that they were intimately connected. I've been so focused on myself that I didn't give a lot of thought to what their lives were like before they arrived at the dig. I'm half-glad that Leo's dad is questioning them, but also a little concerned by it.

"You're from Washington?" Mr. Stamatakis continues with his line of questioning.

Zeke and Lorraine answer his questions politely but provide very little real information about themselves. At first my mom appears puzzled by the direction of his questioning, but she soon becomes obviously ticked off that he is so focused on them personally.

"You seem inordinately interested in the personal lives of my graduate students," she interrupts. "I thought you wanted to know what Leo is doing on the field study. I'm happy to answer any further questions you have about our program." She's smiling, but it's her college professor smile that brooks no argument.

"Of course. I apologize if I appeared to be prying." Mr. Stamatakis hooks his thumb in Leo's direction. "I just wanted to know about the career path that Leo might follow if he decides to pursue archeology."

Leo has a deliberately neutral expression on his face and doesn't meet anyone's eyes.

For the next several minutes, my mom tells Mr. Stamatakis about the Mississippian culture we're studying and the artifacts we've found at the site. She also gives him a thorough explanation of the different career paths that Leo could take. I think by the end he's probably sorry he mentioned it.

We've mostly finished eating and are preparing to get up from the table when I decide to be blunt and ask the question that's been bothering me since Mr. Stamatakis showed up in the United Energy van. "What were your meetings with United Energy about?"

Mr. Stamatakis finishes drinking from his paper cup and sets it down on the table before answering. Maybe he was expecting the question.

"I'm with the US Department of Energy. As you may know, the current administration is very supportive of natural gas as a clean energy source. We were discussing United Energy's plans to expand its fracking operations in southern Indiana."

"You have to know that most of us here are opposed to fracking. Mr. Houseman conveniently attended the informational meeting we held on Saturday about the dangers of fracking," I say in a cold voice.

"We didn't come here to cause any trouble, although we do think that you're spreading misinformation about the so-called dangers of fracking. Reading a few internet articles doesn't make you experts." He holds up his palms in a mollifying gesture, but his tone is just shy of patronizing. "Companies like United Energy are helping to move us away from coal and oil and toward the natural gas that we have right here in the United States."

"And in the process, poisoning our aquifers and releasing methane gas into well water," I counter.

The silver-haired United Energy representative speaks up for the first time. "There is no evidence of that, young lady."

I hate when adults use the term "young lady" as though I'm not mature enough to know what I'm talking about. I'm about to retort, but Scott seizes on this statement and lunges toward him across the table.

"That's where you're wrong." He points his finger at Mr. Stamatakis and Mr. Houseman. "There's plenty of evidence that the chemicals used in fracking are known carcinogens and that they contaminate both the water in wells and aquifers as well as the air surrounding the evaporation tanks. And I've done far more research than just reading a few internet articles. Companies like United Energy have been actively suppressing the evidence and putting gag orders on residents—like the Pennsylvania farmer from our meeting—in exchange for providing drinking water to replace the well water they've contaminated."

"Now let's just hold on a minute," Mr. Stamatakis begins, but I interrupt him.

"No, you hold on. Not only does fracking contaminate the aquifers, but you're also using clean water that gets contaminated in the process. During a time when most of the western states are experiencing extreme drought." I'm so angry at this point I'm struggling to keep my voice under control.

Mr. Houseman leans toward me across Leo and Mr. Stamatakis. "There's an example of where you're misinformed. The water used is reclaimed water, and it's treated and purified before being reintroduced into the water supply."

Leo's dad places a restraining hand on Mr. Houseman's shoulder. "Let's try to stay calm here." But we're way past that point.

"As if it matters that the water is reclaimed," I snap back.

Scott stands up and his hands are shaking as he picks up his cup of water. "It's unconscionable that companies knowingly continue harmful, even deadly, practices, all in the name of corporate profits. Companies like United Energy have known for decades that burning fossil fuels releases greenhouse gases, which can be directly linked to global warming and climate change. But you've hidden that information and tried to discredit anyone who claims it's true. Now you're doing the same thing with fracking."

He flings the water in his cup into Mr. Houseman's face. "How would you like it if that was fracking water? Or contaminated well water that came out of your tap?" He steps over the bench to leave. "I don't know how you can live with yourself." He scrapes off his plate into the trash bin, sets it in the growing pile of dirty dishes and storms off.

Silence follows Scott's outburst, and the rest of us regard the two men with a mixture of disdain and curiosity and wait to see how they'll respond to the accusations. Mr. Houseman blots the water on his face and hair with a napkin and flushes a dark red from the open collar of his shirt to his hairline. Leo sits rigidly, looking as if he'd like to vanish into thin air if he could. Mr. Stamatakis remains composed for the most part, but his lips are pursed in irritation.

When the silence starts to get uncomfortable, and it's obvious that none of us are going to say anything or in any way apologize, Mr. Stamatakis says, "We had hoped to have an opportunity for an open discussion about the positive aspects of fracking, but I can see that emotions are high. Perhaps that was a misplaced expectation. I'm sorry if we disrupted your dinner or upset anyone. Please accept my apologies."

My mom says, "You have a lot of nerve coming here to try to push your agenda on us. There are no positive aspects of fracking to discuss." She stands up from the table. "We very much enjoy having Leo on the field study, but I think it's time for you and Mr. Houseman to leave." She pats Leo on the back and gives him a warm smile. "If you'll excuse me now, I have some work to do this evening." She inclines her head toward Mr. Stamatakis, effectively dismissing him, and leaves to go back to the staff dorm.

We all get up, and Zeke and Lorraine turn to leave as well. I put my hand on Leo's shoulder and give it a squeeze as a way of saying no hard feelings, but he shakes it off and gives me a thunderous look.

I snatch my hand away and take a step back. "Scott and I'll do the cleanup."

"Thanks." He looks at his dad out of the corner of his eye.

As I walk away, Mr. Houseman gets in one last parting remark. "United Energy is already fracking wells in southern Indiana; we have been for years. We're ramping up operations now and getting a lot more landowners to sign over the mineral rights to their land. You can't stop it. It's already happening."

I'm wishing I could go back and punch him in the face, but it's only a fleeting thought.

"Just watch us," I say instead.

Anger still simmering, I gather the rest of the plates off our table and scrape them into the trash can, then hit the other tables to pick up any trash left behind by the other students. Leo and the two cronies leave the shelter and walk toward the parking area. I vent some of my anger by kicking several of the trash cans. Scott has taken the now empty serving bowls for the salad and bread, so I stack the spaghetti bowls and bring them into the kitchen. I fill the sink with soapy water and start washing the pans and utensils.

"Hey, sorry about getting pissed out there. I shouldn't have done that." Scott rinses off sets of tongs and a colander and dries them with a dish towel.

"No, you should have done it. We have to stand up to those guys." I'm up to my elbows in suds. I think I used a little too much dish soap.

He cracks a smile. "That's for sure." He puts the dish towel down on the counter and turns serious. "Sometimes I just want it all to stop, though, you know? The constant battling against these huge corporations and all the crap they throw at you . . . it's discouraging to say the least, and sometimes even dangerous, like what happened at the coffee shop and at your farm. You wonder if fighting it really makes any difference in the long run, if it's really worth it."

"I know I've just joined the battle, but I'm glad my family is fighting them. Even though it can be nasty, I think we have to keeping going. We can't settle for the alternative." I remember the vision from Greystone Mountain of Earth destroyed. "When we push against the big guys, they push back, but we won't give in or give up. I know you've made a difference in Kansas, and you're already helping us here." I say this as much to convince myself as Scott.

"I hope so," he says.

When I've finished washing the last pot, I drain the sink and wipe down the counters. Scott is putting everything away, so I take the trash bag from the kitchen and pick up the bag from the shelter and carry them both to the trash cans behind the old farmhouse.

As I approach the trash cans, I hear Leo's voice coming from the parking area. There's an overgrown hedge separating me from the parking lot, allowing me to hear what's being said without being seen. I stop and gently set down the trash bags. I know I shouldn't eavesdrop, but I want to hear what Mr. Stamatakis has to say.

"Why did you have to bring him along with you?" Leo says angrily.

I assume he's referring to Mr. Houseman, United Energy asshole.

I hear feet crunching on the gravel drive. "Dr. Horton is my professor, and the others are my friends. When I told you what was going on, I didn't think you'd show up and antagonize them."

"That was probably a mistake," Mr. Stamatakis says. "I thought we could have a discussion about fracking, but they're intractable in their opinions. It didn't go the way I'd hoped."

"No kidding. And the way you were questioning Zeke and Lorraine—you could have been more subtle about it. I'm pretty sure you made them suspicious."

"Yes, well, that may not be a bad thing," Mr. Stamatakis counters. "We need to find out what's really going on here. It's a matter of national security. I'm counting on you to keep me informed."

A matter of national security? WTF?

I wait on the path until I hear the doors slam and the van's tires crunch on the gravel as they drive away, then I quietly lift the trash can lids and throw the trash bags inside. I peer cautiously around the corner of the hedge to be sure Leo has left. No sign of him.

I jog back to the dorm. I need to talk to Zeke and Lorraine.

17

ERIC IS IN my room with Renee when I arrive. I'm glad. I think the three of us need to go together to talk with Zeke and Lorraine about what happened this evening with Mr. Stamatakis and Leo. I tell them about Mr. Stamatakis's excessive interest in Zeke and Lorraine at dinner and report what he said to Leo in the parking lot about this being an issue of national security and how Leo should keep him informed.

"Obviously Leo told his dad about Zeke and Lorraine and what they're trying to do," I say. "He may have put them in danger. We'd better go see them."

"It could be part of what's supposed to happen," Renee remarks. "We shouldn't jump to the conclusion that it's a bad thing. Zeke and Lorraine did include Leo in the meditations."

Is this the role Zeke said Leo was going to play?

"It can't be a good thing to have the government poking around, asking questions about them," I say as we leave the room. I wonder once again exactly why Zeke and Lorraine are including him. Why do they want him involved if it puts them in danger? Why do I still want him involved? Am I being naïve in hoping that he'll come around to my point of view?

We cover the distance to the staff dorm in a few minutes. It's the golden hour of the evening when the sun is low in the sky to the west, casting a warm glow over everything and creating elongated shadows. Students aren't supposed to barge into the staff dorm uninvited, so I open the screen door and rap my knuckles on the interior door. Dr. Fraser answers, his glasses perched on the end of his nose and an open book in his hand.

"Hello, kids, what can I do for you? Looking for your mom?" he asks.

"No, we're looking for Zeke and Lorraine. Are they around?" I reply.

"Sure, I'll get them for you." Since the air conditioning is on, he closes the door behind him as he disappears back inside.

After a moment Zeke opens the door, followed by Lorraine. They step out onto the stoop with the four of us. Zeke's wide mouth breaks into a broad smile when he sees us. "To what do we owe the pleasure of this visit?"

"We need to talk to you," I tell them. "Is there somewhere we can go?"

"It's fairly private behind the building near the stream, if that's what you mean." Lorraine looks back and forth between our faces and must see our concern registered there. "Has something happened?"

"You could say that." I tell them what I overheard in the parking lot as we walk around the building to the grassy patch by the creek.

"Leo knows what we're doing and must've told his dad. He's never been truly on board with it. His dad works for the government, and his comment about this being an issue of national security has us worried. I don't know what to think, but you might be in some sort of danger," I say.

"Leo is on his own path and we have to let it play out. I don't think we're in any real danger," Lorraine says.

"At least he doesn't know about the crystal," I reply.

"What crystal?" Eric asks.

"Marcie found a rose quartz crystal with the Sacred Triangle carved into it in her section of the dig on Monday," Renee answers.

"Is it something important?" Eric looks from Renee to Lorraine. "What's the Sacred Triangle?"

"It's the symbol of the partnership between the Ascended Masters, the Light Workers, and the Native cultures as they guide and assist Earth in this age of enlightenment," Lorraine says.

"It could be that we're supposed to use the crystal at some point, but we don't know how—yet. It contains powerful energies and maybe encoded messages. You can feel it when you hold it," I add.

"Where is it now?" Eric asks.

"I put it in with the other artifacts for safekeeping. Anyway, I'm still concerned about Mr. Stamatakis. What should we do?"

"We keep moving forward with our agenda. That's what we do," Eric says.

"Is there enough time? What if we're too late?" I ask Lorraine. A sense of urgency to be doing something wells up inside me, in direct contrast to what they've been saying. It's hard to believe that just thinking about something can make it happen.

"There's still time. Many different outcomes are still possible for the future of Earth, but one of the strongest ones is the raising of human consciousness to allow for ascension to the Fifth Dimension." Lorraine pats me on the back. "Know that what you are doing matters. It matters a great deal."

18

On Saturday, the six of us take a road trip to Grand Caverns National Park. The parking lot is already half-full when we arrive. I hop out of the car onto the asphalt and twist my torso from side to side to get the kinks out of my back. A green bus boasting the slogan *Grand Caverns National Park ~ Powered by Clean Natural Gas!* lumbers past on the road encircling the parking lot.

"Now that's rather ironic, I have to say," Renee remarks.

Leo picks up on our conversation. "I'm telling you, natural gas is the future." He elbows me in the ribs.

After what happened with his dad and the United Energy guy this week, I've been wary of Leo. I want to trust him, but I'm not sure if I should. Of course, I still like him, which puts me in a difficult position. Can I continue to be with him when we disagree on issues that are so important to me?

"I can only hope and do everything in my power to prove you wrong," I answer. "My dad's having a lot of success in spreading the word to property owners, so we'll see how your friends at United Energy like that." I didn't mean to come off sounding so combative, but there it is.

Leo's smile fades and is replaced by a frown. "They're not my friends."

I feel a slight twinge of guilt for calling him out, but I decide to leave it. Our tour of the cave starts at eleven, so we have just enough time to join the other tourists before boarding one of the buses to take us to the cave entrance. We gather off to the side of the tour group, somewhat intentionally separating ourselves from the rest. All the tourists are chattering loudly, so only our group can hear Lorraine when she says, "We'll stay with the tour until we get to the large cavern. Don't be afraid of what might happen. You are perfectly safe."

Is that meant to be reassuring? What is she talking about? Renee looks at Eric in alarm, but he simply shrugs. I want to ask Lorraine exactly what she means, but there isn't time. We're the last ones to get on the bus and take seats in the front.

"What's going to happen?" Leo says to me quietly when we're seated.

"I don't know anything either." I'm not sure why Zeke and Lorraine are being so secretive about what we're doing here. It's hard not to be apprehensive. There's also the added fact that I'm claustrophobic. Just the idea of going into the caves makes me jittery, but I haven't said anything about it. I can handle this. I take a few deep breaths. "I trust Zeke and Lorraine. We'll just have to see what happens."

The tour bus deposits us in a clearing at the side of the road. There's a paved area with stairs that lead down through a large depression in the tree- and scrub-covered hillside to the cave. It isn't the main entrance. This opening has a built-up entrance with a revolving door just inside. Our guide says it's to maintain the air pressure and temperature inside the cave. It's a bit incongruous to see a concrete rectangle with a door in it standing in the middle of the forest, like our own phantom tollbooth. Before we go inside, our tour guide stands on a little raised platform and gives us some basic information.

"Behind us is a natural sinkhole in the forest that funnels water down into the entrance of the cave. During heavy rain, large amounts of water can flow into the cave entrance and down the passages."

Great. I look up at the sky, but it's a cloudless day, fortunately. I don't think I could handle claustrophobia *and* water cascading past me.

"The cave system is at a constant temperature of fifty-four degrees and 80 percent humidity regardless of the surface temperature. Oxygen enters the cave through thousands of tiny fissures in the rock, so we don't have to worry about running out of air!" she says happily.

One less thing to worry about. I'm getting more nervous as the time to enter the cave approaches. I follow Eric and Renee through the revolving door and see a set of very steep and very narrow stairs leading directly down through solid rock. My stomach clenches and I stop and take a deep breath.

"Are you OK?" Behind me, Leo places a reassuring hand on my shoulder. "I could go first if you want."

"Actually, I think it's better if you're behind me." I put my hand over his and put my foot on the first step.

The stairway is narrow and twisting, but it's not as bad as I thought it would be, as long as I don't think about all the rock between me and the surface. Lights are spaced evenly along the metal staircase, and I distract myself by trying to imagine who carried all the steel and electrical wire into the cave to build the stairs and light system in the first place. The guide wasn't kidding about the water. The walls of the cave are damp and dripping in some places, and little streams of water flow from the dark reaches over our heads down to illuminated pools below.

Our pace is unhurried to allow for the slowest of the group to keep up. Leo takes the opportunity during the many pauses in our progress to squeeze my arm or run his hand down my back, which I find reassuring.

When I finally arrive at the bottom of the staircase, I step into an open area with the rest of the group. The ceiling rises at least fifteen feet over our heads, and the walls are more than ten feet away on either side. Both are covered with glistening rock formations. The sound of constant dripping surrounds us. A large drop lands squarely on my forehead, startling me, but the anxiety that I'd been feeling during the descent through the narrow passageway eases.

Our guide is chatting with the people at the front of the group. She waits until the last person steps off the stairs to begin her next presentation.

"The area we're in now is the wet part of the cave, as you can see." She indicates the pools of water on the pathway. "All of these formations have been made by the constantly dripping water depositing minerals and building up stalagmites and stalactites over thousands of years."

The formations are beautiful; they remind me of the drip sand castles we made as kids on vacation at the beach. She continues with her description of the cave, but I stop paying close attention. I don't think this is the large cavern. Lorraine turns toward me and shakes her head. Leo's arm brushes against mine, and he reaches for my hand, entwining our fingers. I love that he's so comfortable being demonstrative in this way. I clasp his hand tightly in mine.

"The water created the caves by gradually dissolving the limestone. There are underground rivers at the very lowest levels of the cave," the guide is saying. "One of the rivers, aptly named the River Styx, comes to the surface out of a wall of rock in the park and joins the Green River and eventually the Ohio River." I find this interesting given our concern about how underground aquifers are affected by fracking.

"We'll be walking for a while through the wet section of the cave, then the rest of the journey will be in the dry section. A layer of sandstone covers that area, repelling water from the cave. Our next stop will be the large cavern."

Zeke's instructions enter my head: *Stay together at the back of the group once we enter the cavern.* Curiosity overrides my concern about what's to come.

As we walk along the path that winds through the cave, the graceful rippling of the walls in the wet portion of the cave gives way to angular, chiseled blocks of smooth rock. Boulders perch precariously on ledges, and cascades of smaller rock falls spill to the cave floor. The dripping slows and eventually stops altogether.

Each time we leave a section of the cave the guide at the back of the group switches off the lights, plunging the path into darkness behind us. For some reason, I imagined the caves as miles of continuously illuminated pathways. Now I realize that was silly. There's no reason to light an empty cave.

The large cavern is unmistakable. It's a huge space, like an auditorium, and the lights fixed to the wall near the path at the front don't fully illuminate the height of the ceiling or the full distance to the far wall. The guides have the group stand together in the front of the room. The six of us move toward the back of the cave.

"Now we're going to do a little experiment. Everyone standing still and stable? OK! Ready . . . now!"

We're plunged into pitch black darkness, a darkness like nothing I've ever experienced before; it almost has substance or weight to it. I can't see my hand in front of my face or even the movement of my hand as I wave it back and forth. The silence is also stunning in its completeness. Even in a small town there are always sounds: birds, crickets, planes and cars, the hum of the furnace and electrical gadgets, neighbors calling. Now the only sound is the shallow breathing of thirty bodies.

I reach to hold Leo's hand for reassurance. Without visual cues to focus on, I feel off balance, like I might fall.

A surge of energy jolts me, and my body starts vibrating from head to toe. I'm not exactly falling, but I have the sensation of movement, and my feet no longer feel like they're connected to the earth. One moment I'm holding hands with Leo, and the next moment I'm disconnected, by myself, alone . . . but, in a way, more connected than I've ever been in my life. It's like I'm linked to all things here in the absolute darkness. Instead of fear, I feel joy.

As suddenly as this sensation started, it ends, and I'm back with my feet on the ground, holding Leo's hand. I'm disoriented because it's still utterly dark, but I sense the others around me. What just happened?

19

"SHIELD YOUR EYES." Zeke's voice booms out of the darkness. "We've brought you to the crystal caves deep in the earth below the underground rivers. The light will be intense at first."

I let go of Leo's hand and cover my eyes. I peek through my fingers and see a dozen glowing white orbs floating in the air above us, gradually growing brighter. As the light increases, it's reflected off the thousands of crystals embedded in the walls and ceiling and erupting from the floor in a myriad of shapes and sizes. Many of them are much larger than the rose quartz crystal I found at the dig. At first the effect is almost blinding, like being at the center of an enormous crystal chandelier.

My eyes adjust to the light, and I look around the space. It's breathtakingly beautiful. Most of the crystals are clear, but some glimmer in jewel tones of amethyst and cobalt and rose. I'm very disoriented, stunned to find that I'm no longer in the large cavern. I sit down on an outcropping of rock to collect myself.

"What did you do to us?" Leo squints as his eyes adjust to the light, and he shakes his head as though trying to reorient himself. "How did we get here?"

"We used teleportation to move you from the large cavern to this cavern. The action is similar to how we're able to move large objects like the stone on Greystone Mountain," Zeke answers.

"Why are we here?" Eric asks.

"Caves are free from the man-made energy waves of TV, radio, microwaves, and other influences that constantly bombard us," Lorraine says. "They also serve as portals to other dimensions."

"Other dimensions?" Renee's voice comes out in a squeak. She reaches out a hand to steady herself on a cluster of purple-tinged crystals on the wall beside her.

"The veil between worlds is very thin here. We're much closer to the Fifth Dimension," Lorraine says.

"You could have told us what you were going to do. I'd like to think that I have a choice in what's going on here." Leo has his arms crossed over his chest, and his face is creased in a scowl.

"We wanted to bring you to this part of the cave to show you the crystals and expose you to their healing and transformative energy. Also, we wanted you to have the experience of teleportation before what comes next."

"What's that?" Leo asks.

"We've not told you everything about ourselves," Lorraine says. She and Zeke exchange a glance. "We have studied with the Native cultures of Earth, but we are more than that. We are Star Beings. We come from the Arcturus star system."

Silence hangs in the air for several minutes. I wonder if the stunned expression on the faces of the others is reflected on my own face.

"So you're extraterrestrials?" Eric says. "As in . . . from outer space?"

"Yes."

At first my mind can't fully absorb this new revelation. First they showed us telekinesis, telepathy, communication with animals, and healing touch. Now they're telling us they're Star Beings from another planet. How can I believe something so outrageous?

"How do we know what you're saying is true? That you're really from outer space," Leo asks, his arms still crossed over his chest. "For starters, how did you get here? Do you have a ship? And why doesn't everyone know you're here?"

For once, I feel the same way as Leo. All the times I went stargazing with my dad I wondered about the stars and galaxies we saw. I felt a certainty that life existed elsewhere in the universe. I never once imagined I would meet that life, though.

"The Arcturian ship the *Athena*, named after your Greek goddess of wisdom for this Earth mission, is in the Jupiter corridor between Jupiter and Saturn. There are many ships belonging to other Fifth Dimension beings there as well, including the Pleiadians, Sirians, and Andromedans," Zeke answers. "You can't see our ships because Earth and humanity are in the Third Dimension. We travel through space and time using consciousness—thought energy—to harness the magnetic resonance energy of the Unified Energy Field and to interface with the powerful computers on our starship. We want to take you to visit our starship, the *Athena*. But it is your choice whether to go or not."

Wow. Fear and excitement race along my nerves, battling for control.

"If we can't see Fifth Dimension beings, then how can we see you?" I ask.

Lorraine answers. "We have the ability to manifest in the Third Dimension if we wish. There is some degree of difficulty, as Third Dimension energy is much denser than that of the Fifth." She hesitates as if considering what to say next and runs her hands along the length of her braid.

"There is also an element of risk to us. A Fifth Dimension being can become entangled in Third Dimension energy and have a difficult time returning to the Fifth Dimension. Zeke and I volunteered to come and help you. If we had been born as humans on Earth in the usual life cycle, we would be subject to karmic influences and likely become trapped in the Third Dimension energy of Earth. We have special protections against entanglement from the Galactic Council that oversees the galaxy. You will meet some of them when we travel to the *Athena*. It's a rare privilege."

"You look human. Did you just appear on Earth in this human form? Are you really human?" Eric leans forward with his elbows on his knees as if to get a closer look at them.

"Essentially, yes. We've taken human forms, but we retain much of our Arcturian characteristics as well," Lorraine answers. "Because we have our Arcturian abilities, the Third Dimension's restrictions of time and space don't constrict us. We can dematerialize at will, so we aren't in danger from your shadow government."

Even knowing this, I still can't discern any difference in their appearance from any other human being. They look completely normal.

"Lorraine and I and all of the higher dimension Star Beings can only offer guidance and assistance. We cannot interfere in Earth's karma because this is a freewill planet." Zeke turns to Leo. "You asked why we don't make ourselves known to all Earthlings, why you don't know about Star Beings. Many in your government do know about us but wish to keep that knowledge a secret. We will not make ourselves fully known until Earth is ready. Our intention is to aide you in your spiritual growth, not to interfere."

Zeke sweeps his arm in an arc encompassing all of us. "The four of you incarnated at this important juncture in Earth's evolution to be part of this mission. You are all Starseeds. Light Workers."

Holy shit.

"We're just a few teenagers. How can we help the entire Earth?" I ask.

"All beings, including all of you, are vastly more powerful than you realize. Zeke and I are here to teach you. When it's time, you'll be ready, and you will know what to do. Earth is in a crisis stage, and you and other Light Workers must act to save her."

"I want to go to the *Athena*." I move away from Leo to sit down beside Lorraine.

He's still glowering off to one side. To hell with him. He and Renee can be freaked out and pissed off if they want, but I'm open to whatever comes, no matter how terrified I am.

"I know you do." Lorraine smiles and places her hand on my knee. She turns back to the rest of our group. "Please have a seat, and we'll tell you about the crystals in this cave and what to expect on the *Athena*. Then you can choose whether or not you want to teleport to the ship."

"You mean now?" Renee asks, alarmed. "Are we going to the ship now?"

Lorraine and Zeke exchange another glance, and Zeke nods as though they've communicated something between themselves.

"I think teleporting to this cave and learning we are Star Beings is enough for today. We'll travel to the *Athena* in the next few days," he says.

Renee visibly relaxes, and the knot of fear and excitement in my stomach uncoils slightly.

"What's the shadow government?" I risk a glance at Leo, but he shows no reaction.

Nothing about a "shadow government" sounds good.

"There are people in your government and other countries' governments who know about extraterrestrials," Zeke says. "They've been contacted by Fourth Dimension beings who gave them advanced forms of technology in exchange for access to the genetic codes of Earth's species. These Fourth Dimension extraterrestrials—or the Greys, as they are often called—are not acting in the highest interest of humanity or the galaxy. They're not part of the Galactic Council. Their species is dying, and they are trying to salvage their race using Earth genetics."

"You mean like harvesting DNA from animals?" Renee grimaces.

"Yes. The practice has been stopped by the Galactic Council, but the Fourth Dimension technology had already been provided to Earth's shadow governments. The government activities are clandestine and only revealed on a 'need-to-know' basis. Not even the US president has had access to what goes on since as far back as Eisenhower, though not for lack of trying. Your President Kennedy may even have been assassinated for threatening to expose them."

"There really are government conspiracies," Renee says. "My dad always says there are, but it's too dangerous to try to expose them." She scoots closer to Eric.

"We didn't tell you this to make you afraid." Zeke's palms are together as if in prayer, and he raises his fingers to his lips. "The Galactic Council, headed by Sananda—who you know as

Jesus—is watching over and protecting Earth along with other beings of light and higher vibration. The immediate danger is that extraterrestrial technology is being used by governments for military purposes. This is not acceptable from a cosmic perspective because the wisdom and spirituality of humanity as a whole has not kept up with their technological and military achievements. There is a definite possibility that those in possession of this technology could unwittingly destroy the Earth."

This is far bigger than pollution or fracking.

"How the hell are we supposed to stop something like that from happening?" Eric throws his hands in the air.

"You are not the only Light Workers on Earth. Many, many people, especially young people, are waking up to the realities of the universe and spiritual consciousness. All over the planet people are connecting, meditating, praying, and sharing their thoughts and ideas. We've told you thoughts are powerful. They are the most powerful thing in the universe. It's contrary to your hard work ethic here in the Third Dimension, but you can create change just by holding positive energy and sending out positive thought patterns. The more people who combine their energies, the more powerful it becomes."

"Why don't you just come to Earth and fix it yourselves?" Renee asks. "You could do it, couldn't you?"

"Yes, there are advanced technologies that could clean up nuclear waste and pollution, repair the damage to Earth's atmosphere." A frown creases Zeke's forehead. "However, it would not solve the problem of the negative forces at work on Earth, which threaten to destroy humanity and the planet. As Earth is a freewill planet, karmically we are not permitted to intervene on that scale. The way we're helping is to work with Light Workers like you. We cannot forcefully change the hearts of men, but you can be a catalyst of change."

"Does anyone else see symbols and what look like mathematical equations streaming across their vision?" Eric asks. "I don't understand their meaning, but somehow I'm getting a sense of information downloading to me."

"Yeah, I'm getting it," Leo says. "I thought I was having a calculus flashback."

"You're picking up on the data stored in the crystals. Thousands of years ago, very advanced civilizations lived on Earth, the civilizations of Lemuria and Atlantis. They achieved very high spiritual and technological mastery and worked closely with Star Beings from Sirius and the Pleiades. However, not everyone was on the path of the light, and some used the technology to control others and grow their own power. It caused the eventual destruction of Atlantis and Lemuria." Lorraine's golden aura shimmers and ripples around her as she gestures.

"Some were tasked with protecting the spiritual and technical knowledge so it wouldn't be lost to future civilizations. They created libraries of information in different parts of the world, in Egypt and the Yucatán peninsula and along the Mississippi River. This is one of those libraries. These crystals hold the secrets that could both save and destroy humanity. When mankind is ready to receive the information, they will find it."

"Now you're telling us that Atlantis was real?" Leo says. "I guess it's no more incredible than Star Beings on Earth." I hope he's considering going to the starship. I can't imagine having this opportunity and choosing to stay behind.

"Yes, it existed for thousands of years," Zeke says. "Many people who lived in the time of Atlantis have reincarnated at this time, which accounts for the duality of light and dark forces at work on Earth today. The struggle is playing out again today with the same potential for positive or disastrous resolution."

"Are we supposed to do anything with the information stored here?" Eric asks. "Because I'm not getting any clear idea what it all means exactly."

Lorraine turns toward Eric. "No. For now, you'll receive the information that you need subconsciously."

Leo has relaxed enough that he's at least sitting down off to one side, but he still has his arms folded over his chest.

Lorraine continues, "The crystals are also imbuing you with their healing qualities and activating certain genetic codes."

"Is the rose quartz crystal I found at the dig site from this cave?" I ask. "Could it have stored records or activation codes?" Maybe we're supposed to get information from it.

"It's possible that it came from here," Lorraine says.

I harrumph under my breath in response to her vague answer. This must be one of those things I'm supposed to find out for myself.

"Now we'll transport back to the main cavern. Tomorrow night we'll meet on Emerald Mound. Those of you who choose to go will travel to the Arcturian starship *Athena*," Zeke says.

I steal a glance a Leo. His face is shuttered, eyes downcast, so I can't get a read on how he's feeling. But the vibe I'm getting from him is mixed. He's still angry, but maybe curious as well; I'm not sure. *Will he choose to go?*

I know one thing. *I'm* going.

"Prepare yourself to be transported." Zeke's words ring out.

The vibrating sensation starts in my chest and moves along my limbs out to my fingers and toes, accompanied by the now familiar surge of energy. An abrupt movement to one side catches my eye. Leo is reaching behind his back to grasp a piece of crystal. His body blocks the view of his movements from the others, but I'm standing slightly behind and can see clearly as he sharply wrenches the crystal downward, snapping it off at the base. He quickly slides it into his pocket. It's the last thing I see before the world goes black and I'm whirling through time and space, all thought whisked from my mind.

20

I'M IN COMPLETE darkness, but I no longer feel like I'm traveling through the vortex. My feet are firmly on the ground, although I'm a little disoriented. Someone is talking.

"Take out your smartphones and turn on the flashlight feature." It's our guide from the cave tour speaking.

We must have arrived back in the cave at the moment we left. I reach into my pocket and pull out my phone. The room lightens slightly as everyone illuminates their touch screens to turn on their flashlights. I turn on my phone's light and it illuminates Renee's face. I touch my own face. *Did I really just travel through space and time?*

"If there were ever to be a power outage in the cave, we could use our smartphones to light our way back to the entrance," our guide says.

Everyone in the group is shining their flashlights around the cavern so the walls and ceiling are brightly illuminated. They do a pretty good job of lighting the cave. I can see that the six of us all arrived back in one piece. Leo looks dazed and unfocused, and Renee looks happy, but maybe she's just happy to be back.

"All of the guides also carry a lighter, which we can use to find our way back, but the smartphones are so much better—as long as the batteries last," the guide continues.

The cave lighting system suddenly switches back on again, and we put our phones away.

"We'll be leaving the cavern through this archway and moving along a series of corridors. Single file and follow me!" The guide leads us through the exit, and the people at the front of the group slowly trail behind her.

We're only a few yards into the tunnel when I feel it. The sensation comes up through the soles of my feet. The earth is vibrating.

At first it's just a slight tremor, but as it grows I also hear a rumbling sound, as if the rock surrounding us is shifting and groaning. The shaking intensifies, and I'm having trouble keeping my balance. The moment I realize what's happening, I'm also shouting, *"EARTHQUAKE!"*

Pieces of rock rain down on us from above, and I put my arms up to protect my head. Zeke sends a shield of blue light over the tour group, and the larger of the rocks bounce off it and tumble to the sides of the tunnel. He seems to be allowing the smaller rocks to penetrate. There's pandemonium in the tunnel as the tourists scream and try to find cover.

"Watch out!" Leo calls to me.

I look up and see that I'm directly in the path of a large rock bumping and rolling toward me at an alarming rate. I think about jumping out of the way, but my legs don't respond. Maybe it won't hurt too much. Why isn't Zeke blocking it? But his attention is turned toward the others.

I face the rock, my hands balled into fists by my sides.

Maybe I can access the Universal Energy Field. I did it before with the log by the stream, but Zeke was helping me. I'm going to try to change the rock's trajectory with my thoughts.

If thoughts are the fastest and most powerful thing in the universe, then I'm using my thoughts for all they're worth. *Zeke! Lorraine!* I can't even formulate a cohesive thought of what I want from them, I just know I need their help. The rock is almost on top of me. I focus on it and imagine it changing course, moving off to my left.

Nothing happens.

The rock is careening toward me. I focus harder.

A tingling sensation flows through my body from my head to my toes like an electrical wave. I feel *more*—like an enhanced version of myself. More aware, more powerful, more confident. OK, maybe I can do this.

The rock moves almost imperceptibly at first, then a little more. Time passes in slow motion. A second stretches until it feels like a minute, a minute like an hour. I reflexively throw up my hands at the last minute to shield my head, but I don't need to. The rock whooshes past me, just grazing my shoulder. It falls harmlessly into the pile of rubble at the side of the path and splits in two. I release my concentration and collapse painfully onto the solid rock of the path.

"Are you OK?" Leo reaches out a hand to help me up.

"Yeah, just some scrapes and bruises," I say, but I'm shaking, as much with shock as incredulity.

Leo pulls me against his chest and runs his hands up and down my back. "I'm so glad you're OK. I thought the rock was going to split your head open." He holds my head in both his hands and kisses my mouth, which unsettles my nerves in another way. "I was so afraid." He pulls away and rests his forehead on mine.

"So was I." I lean back and look into his eyes. "I moved the rock with my thoughts. I think Zeke helped me. And . . . and I think I was tapping into Fifth Dimension energy and the Universal Field."

"If you say so. Whatever it was, I'm glad it worked."

My happiness dims. He doesn't believe me. I pull away from him and smooth my clothes. I'm trying to process what just happened. The broken rock lies harmless on the rubble next to the path. It would have cracked my skull like an egg. I'm probably bruised from falling, but that's it. Somehow I accessed the Field, but I don't know how I did it. I wasn't in full control, and I couldn't have done it without Zeke's help.

I look around the cavern for him and see him on the other side of the path helping some of the others in our group. I catch his eye and send him a mental question.

Did you help me?

Yes, but you could have done it on your own. Zeke's reply fills my head, and he nods at me.

I'm not at all confident that he's right. It didn't feel like I was tapping into the Field when the boulder was barreling toward me. Not until he helped me, at least.

I take inventory of my body. I feel strange, but in a good way. I'm simultaneously grounded by earth and connected to the stars. I sense a power and connectedness I can't fully articulate. Not yet, at least.

The rumbling and shaking continue for several more seconds. Then, just as the rumbling stops, the lights go out, and we're plunged into darkness. A collective cry of dismay and apprehension rises from the group assembled in the corridor. Some people sound close to hysteria. Above it all, the main guide raises her voice to be heard.

"OK, everyone, stay calm. We're going to continue along the path to reach the surface. It's not very far," she calls out. "We'll walk in single file, and every third person should use the flashlight function on their phones to ensure that we have enough battery power to get the entire way back. There may be debris on the path, so watch your step."

Lorraine says quietly, "Don't be afraid. We will get safely out of the cave."

Easy for her to say, but it does help to lessen my fear somewhat.

We line up in single file and make our way through the cave, following the guide. Bits of rock and small boulders litter the ground. We pick our way through the debris by the light of the flashlights. More than half of the group has their flashlights on, ignoring the guide's instructions.

I'm behind Leo, holding on to his belt loops as we walk along the corridor for several hundred yards. In some spots very large rocks have fallen to the floor, and we skirt around them. I'm concerned about possible aftershocks and more rocks cascading down on us. Eventually we reach an opening to a circular staircase heading up but find that it's blocked with a rockfall.

Leo and Eric start clearing the entrance. Most of the rocks are small and easy to lift, but a few are quite large, physically impossible for a couple of guys to move. Eric stands up and looks to Zeke.

Instead of moving them himself, he says to Eric, "You can do this. Access the Universal Field and your own power."

"What about them seeing what we're doing?" Eric motions toward the other tourists.

"I'll shield you so they won't notice."

"OK." Eric shakes out his arms and reaches for one of the large boulders. "I'll give it a try."

"Not me." Leo backs up a few steps. "I wouldn't know where to begin."

"You won't ever be able to connect if you don't begin," Zeke says.

"That's OK. Maybe next time. You and Eric seem to have it covered." He shoves his hands into his pockets.

Zeke sets up a protective shield between us and the other tourists and he and Eric set to work moving the rocks. Zeke easily moves them using his thoughts, tossing them to the side. At first Eric tries to lift one with his hands. He tries picking up a medium-sized rock that still must weigh more than he could normally lift. It budges a little, but he isn't able to move it. When he steps back, his shoulders slump and his arms hang limp by his sides.

"When I accessed the Field before to save my friend Will from a burning car, it was under duress. I didn't have to think about how to do it, it just happened," Eric says. "I'm not sure if I can do it now." He looks dejected.

"Why don't you try using just your thoughts and not your hands." Zeke places his hand on Eric's shoulder. "Close your eyes and focus your mind on moving the rock. I'll give you a little boost." Light flows from Zeke's hand into Eric's shoulder. Eric closes his eyes.

At first the rock just quivers a little and then it rises into the air. Eric is doing it! He opens his eyes to see the rock tumble to the side of the entrance. A broad smile lights up his face and he pumps his fist in the air. After that, it takes just a few minutes for them to move the remaining rocks.

Once the entrance is clear we proceed up the staircase. The lights flicker back on to a collective cheer from the group, but they don't stay on for longer than a couple minutes. We're back to using our flashlights again. I'm not as concerned about being in the cave during an earthquake as I would be if Zeke and Lorraine weren't with us, but I'm anxious to get out as quickly as possible. The claustrophobia is back now that we're on the stairs and only adds to my anxiety.

Suddenly, I feel it—another rumbling in the rock surrounding us—an aftershock.

Instinctively, everyone stops on the stairs and waits. I see the blue light shimmering around us, Zeke's protective shield. Leo puts his arm around me as we wait for the tremor to end. After a few minutes the rumbling subsides, and we continue up the staircase. A woman up ahead of us is sobbing quietly.

I'm beyond relieved when we emerge into the open air. The woods surrounding the exit look unchanged from when we entered the cave. The tour group members stumble out into the sunshine and sit down on the grassy area next to the waiting bus, trying to gather themselves before boarding. Our group meets up next to two large trees. No one is hurt, just shaken up.

"We never have earthquakes around here," I say. "Do you think this could have been caused by increased fracking in the area? I don't want to jump to conclusions, but it's difficult to believe it's a coincidence."

"This area is very near the New Madrid and Wabash Valley fault lines, which aren't very active normally, but the horizontal drilling of fracking is meant to cause cracks in the rocks to release natural gas," Zeke says. "It's reasonable to link earthquakes with the increased fracking activity."

"Scott was saying there's been increased earthquake activity near where he lives, and it's been attributed to fracking," Eric says.

Is this Earth responding to her ill treatment by humans?

Leo is characteristically quiet about what we see as the logical connection between fracking and earthquakes. What is he thinking? Is he starting to understand? I don't really know for sure. I can only hope.

We board the bus for the ride back to the visitor center. The experience of the earthquake has effectively pushed the revelation that Zeke and Lorraine are Star Beings to the back burner in my mind, but it's simmering away for when we're alone and can talk through it.

The visitor center is largely undamaged by the earthquake. We must have experienced the worst of it in the cave. When we arrive back at the car everyone is looking a little more composed.

For the first few miles of the drive home we're all strangely quiet, as though no one wants to be the first to bring up what we just learned—especially with Zeke and Lorraine sitting right in the front seat.

Eric breaks the silence by asking Renee in a low voice, "What do you think about Zeke and Lorraine being Star Beings?"

They're sitting in the back row. I don't think Zeke and Lorraine can hear them, but they can probably read their thoughts. Or do they only do that if we allow it? It's all so strange and confusing . . . and unreal.

I turn around to face Eric and Renee and listen in on their conversation.

"I guess I'm glad, but I'm also even more apprehensive," Renee says. "I mean, it's sort of scary and so outside my comfort zone. And we were in real danger during the earthquake. The whole cave could have collapsed!"

"It's definitely strange meeting actual Star Beings. Even saying those words feels weird." Eric's eyes cut to the front of the car. "But I believe they really want to help us. And I don't think we were in any real danger in the cave. Didn't you see the protective shield Zeke placed over everyone?" I can hear the exasperation in Eric's voice.

"I didn't ask for any of this, and it's really freaking me out." Renee's voice quavers. "I wish you'd have a little more sympathy and understanding for me."

"I'm sorry, babe. I do understand."

"I know how you feel," I put in. "I'm scared, too, and I feel totally inadequate for the task. How are we supposed to change the world? It's an enormous responsibility."

"Yeah, exactly. I'm not sure I *want* to be part of it," Renee says. "I can hardly wrap my head around it, and I can't imagine having an actual conversation with anyone about it. Who would believe me? What would I even say? 'By the way, extraterrestrials are visiting Earth to stop us from destroying ourselves and we could use your help'? This changes our whole worldview and everything we thought was real. Nothing will be the same after this. Everything is turned upside down."

"Yeah, I know." I sit back in my seat, the responsibility weighing heavily on my mind.

Lorraine turns around to face us. "We know this is hard for all of you. No one expects you to take this on all on your own. There are millions of people on Earth who are waking up, and there are a multitude of Star Beings who are supporting them. The most important point for you to communicate is that humans are destroying the Earth in a variety of ways. Then you can teach people the techniques of meditation and shimmering to increase their vibration.

"You'll know who's ready to learn more," she continues. "No one expects you to shout what you know from the rooftops. It's more subtle than that. You will meet people where they are in their ability to take in this knowledge. Also, your simple presence, now that you have this knowledge, helps to elevate the knowledge of others. It's a type of assimilation."

"Back in the crystal cave you said that you volunteered for this mission. Isn't it a hardship to be away from home for so long?" I ask.

"Yes, we volunteered, and it's an honor, not a hardship. The Arcturian life span is hundreds of years, so the time we're spending on Earth is not long in comparison."

"Hundreds of years?" Renee asks.

"Yes, and even when we do 'die,' as you call it, we do not cease to exist. We simply transition to a different vibration where we will begin a new incarnation."

"Just when I thought this couldn't get any stranger, something new comes up to prove me wrong," Eric says. "You're talking about reincarnation, right?"

"Yes, you would call it that," she answers.

"Do we reincarnate too?" Renee's voice is almost a whisper.

"Yes, each of you has lived hundreds, even thousands of lifetimes, some on Earth and some on other planets, and you will live thousands more lifetimes to come."

Renee puts her hands on either side of her head. "OK, I think that's enough information for me to take in right now. It's been a full day."

"Maybe we can just listen to music for now while we let this all soak in," Eric says.

"Sure." Zeke grabs the cord plugged into the stereo. "Do you want to pick the playlist?"

"Even that would be too much." Eric reaches past the middle seats and takes the cord from Zeke's outstretched hand. "I'll just put it on shuffle."

I'm not ready to let this subject go yet. I lean forward to tap Lorraine on the shoulder. "Before we put on the music, I have a question about reincarnation. Why don't we remember our past lifetimes?"

"When you are between incarnations, you do remember all your lifetimes. You use that information in selecting your next lifetime," she says. "Each lifetime is its own learning experience, so remembering previous lifetimes would interfere with that learning."

"OK." I lean back heavily into my seat. "You can put the music on. I'm on overload now too."

I look over to Leo, seated beside me. I wonder what he's thinking.

21

I CAREFULLY STEP over a tangle of roots on the path. It hasn't rained much in the last few days, so the path along the bluff beside the river is hard packed and not muddy, but there are lots of tree roots to watch out for. I try to look up at the scenery as often as possible and not keep my eyes downturned the entire time, but I don't want to trip and fall down the bluff into the river either.

After the bombshell Zeke and Lorraine dropped on us yesterday, I needed something very real and normal to ground me, so I asked Renee if she wanted to hike along the bluff today. Plus we're traveling to their starship tonight, apparently, and I didn't want to spend the day thinking about *that*.

Lainey asked if she could come along with us, too, which is great. I like her and feel like we haven't gotten to spend much time together.

"Whew, it's muggy out today." Lainey stops on the path in front of me and pulls her water bottle from the side pocket of her pack. She takes a deep drink and wipes the back of her neck with her bandana.

I grab my own water bottle and guzzle from it. "At least we're in the shade here." It's a cloudless day, and the sun's rays reflect off the river below, creating a million tiny diamonds in the water that glint and sparkle and dance along with the flow of the current, but on the path we're in the dappled shade provided by the trees.

Renee pushes her sunglasses back over her forehead and wipes her face with her bandana. "Yes, it's nice up here on the bluff. There's a pretty good breeze too," she says.

By tacit agreement she and I haven't talked at all about what happened in the caves yesterday or what we learned. Given how freaked out she was already by what was going on, I can only imagine what this new information has done for her comfort level. I'm not entirely sure how I feel, either. At first what Zeke and Lorraine showed us was incredible and amazing; then it was scary and mind blowing. But now I don't even know what to think. Star Beings. Accessing the Universal Energy Field with my thoughts. *Did I really do that?* I think I just need to process things on a more subliminal level and not consciously analyze everything. A walk in the woods seems like the perfect setting for that.

"Do you guys feel like going further? My GPS says we've already hiked a mile and a half. Want to go another mile and then turn around?" Lainey asks. "That'll be five miles total."

"Sure." I look at Renee, and she nods while swallowing a gulp of water.

"OK, great! I was hoping you'd be up for it. Follow me." Lainey replaces her water bottle and sets out along the path.

We walk silently for a while, enjoying the rhythm of walking, moving past branches and foliage. My biggest concern is brushing up against poison ivy. It's all along the sides of the path. That would not be fun. It would actually totally suck. I have some lotion that's supposed to neutralize the oils that cause the rash. Let's hope it works.

"Crap!" Lainey cries out as she tumbles to the ground on her hands and knees. She rolls over onto her butt and grabs her ankle.

"Shit. I wasn't looking and I stepped in a hole and twisted my ankle." She grimaces and rocks back and forth. "Owww. It really hurts. I think it's bad." She starts to unlace her shoe.

"Wait," I say. "I don't know a lot about first aid, but I do know from running that you're not supposed to take off your shoe when you sprain your ankle. You won't be able to get it back on once your foot starts to swell."

"OK." Lainey's breath comes in short rapid gasps, and her face is pinched with pain.

"Can you walk on it?" Renee asks.

"I don't know. Give me a minute." Lainey was already perspiring from our hike, but now beads of sweat have broken out on her forehead and upper lip.

"Let me see." I gently place my fingers on her hand, which is covering her ankle. She moves it away, and I see that the skin above her shoe is already puffy and swollen and turning a mottled pink.

A thought occurs to me and I look up at Renee. "Do you think I should try healing touch?"

"Can you do that? Have you done it before?" Renee says.

"No, I've just watched Zeke, but I could try."

"Yes, I think it's worth trying," Renee says. Then she adds, "I could try to help." I nod and smile at her. That's a positive sign.

"You can do healing touch?" Lainey asks.

"Well, I'm not sure, but I can try," I say. "Do you know what it is?"

"Yeah, I'm kind of into that stuff. My aunt owns a spiritual bookstore. Some of the practitioners who come to the store have the ability."

"Your aunt owns a spiritual bookstore? That's cool!" How am I just learning this now?

"Is it OK if I try it on you?" I ask.

"Sure! Anything to make my ankle better."

She takes her hands away from her foot and slowly and gingerly stretches her leg out along the path. If anything, the swelling is already worse. Her skin is puffing out over the edges of her shoe and has turned an ugly shade of purple. It's a bad sprain, maybe even something worse. I kneel on the path next to her and Renee sits beside me.

"Ready?" I ask Lainey.

"Yes. Just try not to press too hard," she tells me.

I gently encircle her ankle with my hands, being careful not to apply any pressure. Heat from the injured tissue radiates into my palms, and I even feel some of the pain Lainey must be feeling. A shudder courses through me. I want to simultaneously take away the pain and swelling while also sending healing energy into Lainey's ankle. A sort of two-way exchange of energy.

I close my eyes and take deep, slow breaths from my core. A sense of calm comes over me, and I concentrate on connecting with the flow of energy all around me. My palms start to tingle as I focus on healing thoughts. Lainey must feel something because she lets out a little gasp.

Renee places her hands over mine, and my eyes flicker open briefly at her touch. She leans forward with her head bowed. Warmth flows from her hands into mine, and the tingling intensifies. We sit for several minutes. The only sounds are our synchronized breathing and the humming of crickets.

"Can you feel anything?" I ask Lainey.

"Maybe. I'm not sure. Your hands feel warm, and I feel prickling like pins and needles on my skin."

A rustling and flapping sound comes from the tree above us. I look up and see a red-tailed hawk has landed on a branch not ten feet over our heads.

"Wow," Lainey says. "A hawk totem."

"A what?" Renee asks.

"The hawk. It's a spirit animal message."

"What does it mean?" I ask.

"Let me see if I can remember . . . I think the hawk totem represents leadership, bravery, and intuition . . . and teamwork. Yes, teamwork!" she exclaims. "Maybe I'm supposed to help with the healing, too, and add to the teamwork. Here." She scoots her butt closer to her foot so she can reach her ankle with her hands. "I'll put my hands over yours."

She lays her hands over Renee's and immediately the warmth I was feeling is elevated to actual heat. Combined with the tingling it's almost too uncomfortable to bear, but we stay that way for several minutes, focused on sending healing energy to Lainey's ankle. After a while, the tingling stops, and the heat dissipates, leaving my hands feeling cold and sweaty.

"I think we can stop now," I say. We let go of Lainey's ankle and I shake out my hands.

I look up into the tree and see the hawk is still there. Its black eyes are focused on the surface of the water, watching intently. Suddenly it spreads its wings and arrows toward the river, swinging its talons down at the last minute and plunging them into the water. It rises from the surface with a fish writhing in its claws. It returns to the tree and perches even higher than before, gazing down at us with its prize now twitching against the branch.

"That was so cool!" I exclaim.

"Yes, what a beautiful creature," Renee says. She turns to Lainey. "Is that a message as well?"

"I don't know if it's a different message. Maybe just reinforcing the original one." She probes the puffiness around her ankle with her fingers.

"How does your ankle feel now?" I ask. The swelling has gone down, and the ugly purple shade has faded to a light pink.

"Better." She gently moves her foot back and forth. "It feels almost back to normal. It's incredible."

"Yeah, I'm kind of amazed," I say. *We actually did it.*

"Can you walk on it? It's almost two miles to get back." I undo my ponytail to smooth the flyaway hairs back off my face and refasten the hair tie.

"We can walk with you balanced between us, so you don't have to put weight on your foot," Renee says.

"OK. Just give me a few minutes. I think I can do it if we go slow. It does feel better, but I want to be careful."

"Sounds good." I pull out my phone. "I'm going to Google 'hawk totem' and see what comes up." I scroll through several articles, then one catches my eye. I click on it.

"Here's something." I read out loud. "Hawk spirit message can mean that the recipient is a 'Spirit Warrior' and a visionary. Hawks have excellent eyesight and can see both the big picture and small details. If you have hawk as your totem, you have a warrior spirit and will fight for what is right." *Am I a Spirit Warrior? Are all of us?*

When Lainey has rested a bit and gathered her strength, we head back along the trail. She hops along, carefully placing weight on her injured foot. She has her arms looped around Renee's shoulders and mine on either side. It's slow going, giving me plenty of time to consider the meaning of the hawk totem message.

I feel like the message was at least in part for me. What does being a Spirit Warrior involve? What am I supposed to do? Most importantly, is it something that I want?

22

"TONIGHT WE WILL travel to the Arcturian Starship *Athena*—if you choose to," Lorraine says. It's dinnertime, and the six of us are seated at a table by ourselves, but I still look around to see if anyone can overhear us.

Renee shifts uncomfortably on the bench and glances at Eric. He doesn't look up.

"While we're there, you'll have the opportunity to experience the healing chambers we've prepared for you and to meet some of the members of the Galactic Council. You've been given special dispensation to travel to our Fifth Dimension ship even though you are still Third Dimension beings." Zeke shovels a spoonful of chili into his mouth, chews, and swallows before continuing. "We feel the experience will help you as you begin to communicate with other awakening Light Workers. Do you have any questions for us?"

"Are we safe on the starship? Is there any danger that we won't be able to come back?" Renee asks as she unravels a loose piece of string from the hem of her T-shirt.

"It's not time for you to ascend to the Fifth Dimension permanently. You still have work to do here on Earth, so there's no danger of being stuck there or left behind. As for safety, you will actually be safer on the *Athena* than you are on Earth," Lorraine says.

"I'm just not sure. It's scary, you know?" Renee smiles nervously.

"I think you should come," Eric says. "We're all scared."

"Are you going?" She swivels her body to face him.

He nods.

"Even if I don't?" He looks at her for a few beats and visibly swallows.

"Yes, I'm going regardless."

Renee's jaw clenches. Now, instead of being afraid, she's obviously pissed at Eric. She whips her head around to Zeke and Lorraine, her hair swinging out behind her.

"OK, then I'm going." She bites off each word. Maybe being pissed is better than being afraid.

We all look at Leo. He's leaning forward with his forearms propped on the table. He lowers his head and reaches one hand up to rub the back of his neck. When he looks up again his gaze meets mine, and I give him what I hope is a reassuring look.

"Yeah, I'll go too. I'm sure I would regret it forever if I didn't." One corner of his mouth lifts in a faint imitation of a smile.

"All right, we'll meet on Emerald Mound tonight after dark and transport to the starship *Athena* located in the Jupiter corridor," Lorraine says. Just hearing her say it makes a trickle of apprehension roll down my spine.

ZEKE EXTINGUISHES THE lantern he brought, and darkness comes rushing in. It's not the pitch black of the cave, but an enveloping, protective blanket of dark. We're arranged in a rough line along the crest of Emerald Mound. I reach for Leo's hand beside me, and he gives my hand a squeeze. I feel a mixture of fear and anticipation. Is this really happening?

"Prepare yourselves to transport," Zeke says.

I'm sucked into space. Color and light flow through the vortex, creating swirling patterns in the darkness around me. The light changes and begins to stream by me. I'm moving past objects that I can sense but not see. An enormous presence—a pulsing, throbbing energy—comes into my awareness. Could it be Mars? My thoughts aren't entirely coherent, but I think Mars is between Earth and Jupiter. Does a planet have a presence, an energy field?

As I move through space and time, I'm united with everything in the cosmos, connected with all things yet still retaining my individuality. It's indescribably wonderful. Then my body coalesces into the whole of me, and I'm there. I've arrived on the starship *Athena*.

We're in a large, open atrium. Hanging from the arched dome overhead is a sculpture made from shards of glass, sharp and dangerous looking. It chimes with a sound so beautiful it makes me catch my breath and reflects the sparkling light in the room into a rainbow of colors that I can't even begin to describe. The air surrounding us is *sparkling*, filled with glittery flecks like iridescent dust motes.

The colors are saturated and intense, far richer and more vibrant than the colors I'm used to. The walls are deep purple, lit with glowing light from around the edges of the floor and ceiling, but they also pulse with an energy of their own as though somehow the ship itself is a living thing.

Low, rectangular couches in deep shades of russet and gold are arranged together to one side. A woman is seated at a table across from us. At least I think she's a woman. She is so pale that her skin is almost transparent, and her shoulder length hair is silver white. She's gazing at us with wide-set cobalt blue eyes, the blue filling the entire orb. And she's smiling, which I take as a good sign, but no teeth show in her mouth.

The most arresting thing in the room, though, is the wall of windows looking directly out into space. The great hulking mass of what I assume is Jupiter hovers to one side. Several of its moons are visible, suspended in space like colorful marbles in a game of jacks. Jupiter's shifting atmosphere is striated in shades of white and tan and gold. Behind it, filling the expanse of windows, is the vastness of space, black velvet covered with pinpricks of millions of stars. The glowing band of the Milky Way arches across the sky as a dim white glow. Hovering in the area immediately beyond the windows are dozens of spaceships.

It's true. Star Beings have come to our solar system.

The others in our group are as transfixed by the view as I am. Zeke gestures for us to move closer to the window.

Leo links his arm through mine. "I'm sorry I got mad. I almost let my pigheadedness stop me from being here," he whispers in my ear.

I put my hand over his. The flecks of light in the air float between us and surround him in a faerie halo.

"I wouldn't have let you stay behind," I tell him.

He bumps me with his elbow. But I was prepared to go without him. There was no way I was going to miss this.

"Where are all those ships from?" He places his hands on the railing that runs in front of the windows.

The ships are all shapes and sizes, ranging from slim saucers to large circular structures with arms that extend out into satellite orbs. Beyond Jupiter I think I can see the asteroid belt separating it from Mars. As I look more closely at the jumble of rocks zooming past, it comes sharply into focus, and the ships in the foreground become blurry. When I turn my attention back to the ships, they come into focus again, and the asteroids go fuzzy. The window must have some sort of an enhanced magnification property that brings into focus whatever I'm looking at.

Leo swats at the air around him, seemingly annoyed with the sparkling specks. As if in response to his gesture, the air swarms him with even more of the iridescent flecks, like clouds of good-natured gnats taunting and teasing him. When he stops flailing his arms, the specks settle around him, but I get a sense of mirth coming from the air—if that's even possible.

Zeke comes to stand next to Leo at the window. "I see you've already encountered the faerie light." He barely contains his laughter.

Leo smiles back at him. I'm glad he left his negative attitude behind. How could he stay mad, with all this truly out-of-this-world stuff surrounding us?

"I never tire of this view," Zeke says. "The ships are Arcturian, Pleiadian, Sirian, Alanoan, and Andromedan. Higher vibrational beings are very interested in what's occurring on Earth. They want to observe and assist with raising your vibration—and to try to prevent the total annihilation of Earth and her inhabitants. The entire galaxy is helping you, though you are unaware of it. The destruction of Earth would cause disastrous ripple effects throughout the cosmos."

He turns away from the window to face us. "A time will come in the not too distant future when we will reveal ourselves to all of humanity. It will be one of the most significant events to occur in Earth's history. The event will go 'viral,' as you say." He makes quotation marks in the air. "And be seen by billions of people across the planet. It will change everything that humans know about themselves and the universe and have a unifying effect on humanity, creating an upliftment."

It could also cause a lot of fear and chaos.

Zeke looks directly at me. "Yes, there is the potential for a Star Being visitation to create fear and confusion. It's one reason we're working with individual Light Workers to prepare the way." He pauses and places a hand on Renee's shoulder. "You four will be among the Way Showers."

I've become more accustomed to the idea of this responsibility, this role they're asking us to play, but I can't say I feel prepared or capable. What are we supposed to do anyway? The question keeps coming back, and I don't feel like I really have an answer.

Now Zeke sweeps his arms out to each side and bows slightly from the waist. "I should welcome you all to the Arcturian starship *Athena*. The environment here mimics our home on Arcturus, so we don't feel deprived being away. Although you are not fully in the Fifth Dimension yourselves, you will get a sense of what it's like."

He leans against the strut of the window beside him. "The ship is very large—twenty miles in diameter—and has the capacity to work with large numbers of people when the Ascension occurs."

Twenty miles?! The ship would cover more than the entire square mileage of my hometown, including the university.

"The *Athena* is able to respond to our needs and telepathic requests in the same way a computer receives your keystroke commands. We are able to interface directly with our thoughts." He leads us out of the reception area through an arched doorway and down a corridor lined with doors.

The purple walls ripple and glow a brighter lavender color as we pass by, reinforcing my sense of them as alive.

"The meditation rooms are in this section. Other sections have healing chambers and calibration chambers. These are created for each individual who will ascend."

The doors of each room appear as a film of electrical current. Zeke presses a button next to one of the doors and it dissolves out from the center, revealing a room with cushions and a fountain and stream running through it.

At the end of the long hallway is a set of double doors. They look as if they're made of pure gold. The ambient light reflects off their polished surface.

"Now it is time for you to meet with members of the Galactic Council and the Sacred Triangle. The true partnership of the Sacred Triangle is between the Ascended Masters, Native cultures of Earth, and Star Beings." Zeke motions to the doors and they swing slowly open.

At first I can't see clearly because of a brilliant glow at the center of the room. I keep my gaze averted as we enter a circular room with a raised dais in the center. Music fills the air. It reminds me of classical music by Vivaldi or Mozart, but it's even more complex and soul piercing. The walls of the room are covered in a metallic-gold, fabric-like material that is draped and pleated around the entire space. It both reflects the room's light and glows with a light of its own. The same fabric extends to the ceiling, where it's gathered tightly in the center over the dais and covered with a royal blue medallion. Inscribed on the medallion is the intertwined circle and triangle symbol of the Sacred Triangle.

Zeke and Lorraine usher us into seats in front of the dais. The dais appears to be floating in the air with no visible means of support. I feel like I'm about to have an audience with royalty. A long, burnished gold table takes up most of the space on the raised platform. Seated at the table in magnificently carved chairs—you could even say thrones—are what can only be described as beings of light.

I count eleven beings in total. Some, but not all, appear human. Sitting as close as we are, we're in the circle of light emanating from them. I can feel their love and compassion for us in the same way I feel Zeke's thoughts enter my mind. Any fear I had is washed away by the strength of their love. The sparkling motes in the air glitter more brightly in the circle of radiating light and love energy.

At the end of the row stands a man dressed in a Native American style, wearing a fringed and beaded leather tunic and leggings and a white feathered headdress.

"Hey-ho!" he calls to us, his voice deep and resonant. "We welcome you, Light Workers. You honor us with your presence. Your mission is vitally important to the future of our beautiful planet Earth, and we wish to help you."

Not what I expected at all. *They* are honored?

"I am Chief White Eagle, representative of the Native peoples of the Sacred Triangle. We have others here who wish to be known to you. First I will introduce you to the Ascended Masters from Earth. They have taken the human form by which you will recognize them, but they are multidimensional beings and have many forms." He motions to the others seated at the table and beats out a short rhythm on the drum he's holding.

Some of the beings are no more than a faint, translucent holographic image, as though they are not fully present. Others appear more solid in form. Some have very strange forms.

Chief White Eagle continues, "Seated beside me are Osiris and Isis, the Egyptian gods of death and resurrection and of magic and life."

The two are regally dressed in a white gown and white tunic and wear collars of gold inlaid with semiprecious stones. They gaze at us with kohl-ringed eyes and nod in acknowledgment.

"Next at the table are Buddha and Muhammad." Chief White Eagle's drum sounds, *rum-bum-bum.*

This is not the rotund Buddha as we might recognize him from later in his life, but a younger version. He still has the recognizable topknot and is dressed in saffron robes. He brings his palms together in front of his heart and bows to us. I feel prompted to bow in return.

The Prophet Muhammad is dressed in a turban and flowing robes of white, contrasting sharply with his full, dark beard. He also acknowledges us with an incline of the head. It's somewhat overwhelming to be face to face with these mystical beings; I've heard of them all but only half believed they actually existed. I'm glad they aren't speaking. Just being in the room with them and absorbing the huge energies they generate is challenging enough.

Rum-bum-bum, rum-bum-bum, rum-bum-bum. The fringe on the arms of Chief White Eagle's tunic oscillates in time to his beat. "Sananda, or Jesus, as you may know him, asks me to welcome you on his behalf and expresses his gratitude for your work."

Jesus! Jesus is here? He appears as a holographic image suspended in the air, almost translucent and shimmering ever so slightly, three dimensional and fully present, and yet not fully present at the same time. His dark hair is swept back from his face, and his skin is almost the same dusky brown color as Leo's. Like Muhammad, he has a full beard. His deep brown eyes are penetrating, but full of warmth and kindness. Rays of light radiate from the golden aura that surrounds him. He raises both of his arms in front of him with his palms facing us. Great love and compassion flow from him into my mind and heart and soul. It's as though he's placed his hands on my head and over my heart.

My father gives you his love. It's a fleeting thought, a mere wisp of an idea, but I feel sure that it came from Sananda.

"Quan-Yin is also here to welcome you," Chief White Eagle says next.

Beside Jesus is a pale-skinned woman with Asian features and jewels at her neck, ears, and wrists. I'm struck by the diverse backgrounds of the representatives assembled here. Then I look at the being who's seated beside Quan-Yin and realize that, while diverse so far, those introduced to us have all been human beings. This next being is definitely not human.

His skin—if he is a he—is cerulean blue, and not only skin covers his body. He also has lustrous scales that reflect the light in the room with a silvery gleam. He appears to be a mixture of human and amphibian. His face looks human, but he has gills on his cheeks, webbing under his arms and between his fingers, and finlike protuberances on his head and back.

"Representing our Star Being friends from the Sirius star system is Jalulus. You observed the Sirian ships stationed in the Jupiter corridor."

So far no one except Chief White Eagle has said anything beyond giving us a nod of acknowledgment, and no one in our little group of human explorers has had the nerve to say a word. Jalulus also does not utter any words, but as with Sananda, I receive the message of his greeting in my thoughts. Of course, they all must be able to communicate telepathically. As I realize this I'm horrified to think that Jalulus might have read my thoughts of shock, a little bit of fear, and even revulsion when I first encountered him.

A ripple of laughter comes to me from him as this all runs through my mind. *Not to worry, my Earthling friend. You appear strange to us as well, but this is not the first time I have seen a human. Inside we are all the same.*

I send him thoughts of greeting and gratitude, and what I hope is a little humor, in return. As I watch him, his laughter still ringing in my head, his entire body dissolves until just the features of his face are surrounded by blue rings of snapping electricity. I blink a few times in surprise. I can only see his eyes and his smile, but his presence is still strong.

"From the Pleiadian Star System, the Priestess Raneom is here to greet you."

I'm more prepared this time, but still taken aback by the reptilian creature who stands next to Jalulus. Her thick, bumpy skin is multiple shades of green, like a verdigris collage, and changes color as she gives a slight bow in greeting. A slim green and gold snake is wrapped around her upper arm like a piece of living jewelry. She holds us in her gaze, her irises vertical slits. Her powerful tail swishes back and forth on the floor behind her.

"Hey-ho, hey-ho!" Chief White Eagle chants and beats out the rhythm on his drum. "The last two Star Beings present are Seventh Dimension beings. Sophestus from Xenate and Arania from Alano, the moon planet. They have moved beyond the constraints of physical bodies and appear to you in their pure consciousness energy essence."

Beyond Raneom are two shapes that look for all the world like undulating soap bubbles with translucent, rainbow-spectrum colors sliding over the surface. I find it very hard to identify these apparitions as sentient beings, but apparently they are highly advanced, as they have no need for a physical presence. I guess God doesn't need a physical body, either.

"Those of us in the Sacred Triangle and Galactic Council gathered here are just a few representatives of the thousands of Ascended Masters and Star Beings who are watching Earth, supporting your mission, and helping where we can." Chief White Eagle motions to those seated at the table. "We want you to know that while we cannot interfere with the events unfolding on Earth, we are able to mitigate some potential disasters. When nuclear weapons are detonated in space, where they could potentially rip the space-time continuum, we use our technology to contain and alleviate the potential devastation. The same is true when nuclear reactors, like Fukushima, have breaches of radiation. We do what we can to contain the effects of the leaks without interfering to the extent that we would override your free will. Hey-ho, hey-ho, hey-ho," he chants and beats on the drum.

"Researches at CERN using the Hadron Collider are doing very advanced experiments in particle physics, but they do not have the technical and spiritual knowledge to be aware of the impact of their experiments. There is the possibility they may open a very, very large star gate that would allow lower Fourth Dimension energies access to your planet. Star Beings appear at the collider as glowing orbs and disrupt those experiments to prevent such a calamity. There was a time when Star Beings from the Fourth Dimension were allowed access to Earth, but Earth is now under the protection of the Galactic Council. Therefore that activity has been limited, and it is best to keep it that way."

He looks at each of us in turn. "The four of you have access to any of the eleven beings gathered here. You need only ask for our guidance and assistance, and it will be given. As you are still in the Third Dimension, you may not be aware of our presence, but we are always available." Chief White Eagle thrums softly on his drum. "Do not feel that any request is too insignificant or that you may be bothering us. As multidimensional beings, we have the ability to exist on multiple planes, and we wish to support you as you embark on this path."

This all sounds good. I like the idea of having a cadre of spiritual beings at my beck and call, but I still feel inadequate for the task they've set before us.

A brief silence follows his statement, and I feel as though they are expecting some sort of response from us.

I look down our row and no one seems eager to speak up, so I square my shoulders and say, "Thank you for your support and guidance. We greatly appreciate this opportunity and the help you're providing." I'm hoping this is the right thing to say.

Osiris and Isis incline their heads and the Seventh Dimension beings gleam more brightly.

"It is time for the Ascended Masters and Star Beings to take their leave of us, but remember they are as close as a thought. You may find that you identify most with one or another guide, and that is fine." Chief White Eagle plays a slightly different rhythm on his drum—*rum, rum, rum, bum, da-bum, bum, rum, rum, rum, bum, da-bum, bum*—and the beings at the front of the room simply vanish.

The light in the room dims, and the powerful energy of their presence is gone as well. I feel a little bereft at their absence.

"Now we'll give you a brief glimpse of the Fifth Dimension before you return to Earth. We understand that it is difficult to strive to ascend to the Fifth Dimension if you have no concept of what it is like. There are certain requirements you must meet to enter the Fifth Dimension. It is a higher consciousness, so there is no ego, selfishness, jealousy, hatred, fear, or will to dominate. These negative emotions are not permitted in the Fifth Dimension."

Well, that leaves me out of the equation. I still have my share of negative emotions.

"However," Chief White Eagle continues, "those who are working toward spiritual growth are granted the gift of Grace. If you have not yet attained the vibration required to enter the Fifth Dimension at the moment of Ascension, but you have been working toward it, you will be given Grace, what you might call a 'boost,' and you will be allowed to come to the starship *Athena* to complete the process."

He removes a wooden dowel from the folds of his tunic. One end is decorated with white feathers and a beaded band, and the other end tapers to a narrow point.

"In the higher dimensions there is no war and no competition. It is a glorious place of love, acceptance, and higher spiritual energy."

He begins tapping on the wooden edge of his drum in the staccato beat that Zeke used on Emerald Mound and by the stream, *tat, tat, tat, tat, tat, tat.* "We'll be using the shimmering technique you learned from Zeke and Lorraine. Close your eyes and visualize your aura surrounding your body and pulsing in rhythm with the beat of my drum. Faster and faster, raising your vibration."

I close my eyes and see my aura ringed with the purple line of light, vibrating in time with the beat of the drum.

"Imagine your energy body rising out of your physical body, moving to the Fifth Dimension. On the count of three, *shimmer.* One, two, three—*shimmer, shimmer, shimmer!*"

I open my eyes and find myself in a vast library. It's a room without walls or ceiling. Shelves of books rise into the blue of the sky and march off into the distance as far as the eye can see. Beings in blue and white robes move amongst the shelves, or maybe the shelves are moving and rearranging themselves. The beings are all shapes and sizes. One looks like a giant praying mantis, while another could be described as a very furry dog, and a third looks like a blob of green Play-Doh with eyes and a nose.

Orbs of light float through the room, and I'm pretty sure they're beings not in physical form. Round wooden tables line the center of the room, and some of the beings are seated at the tables with huge tomes open in front of them. But it's my own sense of knowing that is so incredible. I find that I have access to all the knowledge in this library . . . and in the universe. I simply ask a question or wonder about something, and the answer arrives in my head. It reminds me of when I was young, when my parents were mad at me for something I didn't do, and I thought that someday they would know the truth. I must have been thinking of, or remembering, this library, where all the records are kept.

"Yes!" Chief White Eagle says as though responding to my thoughts. He's in his physical form, but his skin is smoother, and his eyes are more brilliant. Everything about him is enhanced. The others are also transformed. They look like themselves, but more—more beautiful, more radiant, and exuding good health.

Leo runs his hand through my hair. "It's like liquid silk." His smile is dazzling.

"This is the Hall of the Akashic Records, where all the information in the galaxy is stored. Beings come from every corner of the galaxy to access the records. Look up!" Chief White Eagle points to where the ceiling would be, and a current of wind with visible eddies and ripples flows through the library. "That is the stream of Collective Consciousness, where all of the thought energy of every being in the galaxy flows together. Earth has its own current, one that contains the thoughts of all the humans and other sentient beings on Earth. It is how we are all connected. It is also called the Universal Energy Field or Unified Field because of the powerful thought energy it contains."

I want to stay in the library and absorb all the knowledge it contains. I have so many questions, I don't even know what to ask.

"Next we go to the Crystal Lake." *Rum, ba, rum-bum, rum, ba, rum-bum.*

Again we're swept through time and space.

A pebbly shore surrounds a wide blue-green lake. Hundreds of beings line the shore. Many are like the woman in the atrium, slim and graceful like a ballet dancer, very tall with translucent skin, but there are many others. Most are seated, eyes closed, in the posture of meditation or talking quietly in groups.

"Are we on Arcturus?" Eric asks.

"Yes, the Crystal Lake is on Arcturus. We Arcturians are tasked with caring for it and the energy it generates," Zeke says.

The sun shining in the sky is much larger than our sun, and it has a slightly reddish hue to it. The air sparkles with the faerie dust. This is definitely not Earth.

"We come here to receive energy from the sacred crystal. It is very powerful and must be kept partially submerged to protect us from its intensity," Lorraine says.

At the center of the lake is what looks like a clear iceberg rising sharp and jagged above the water, suggesting an unknown bulk hidden beneath the surface.

"Please sit and receive the healing energy of the crystal." Chief White Eagle indicates the pebbled beach in front of us.

I sit cross-legged on the ground. Zeke and Lorraine sit in front of us. They still look very much human, not at all like the beings surrounding the lake.

"We'd like to tell you a bit about life on Arcturus on the Fifth Dimension," Lorraine says. "Arcturus is different from Earth in many ways yet similar in others. Earth has a vast variety of species of plants and animals and over seven billion people. Arcturus is not nearly as diverse, nor as populated. There are only five million Arcturians. You can see the landscape of Arcturus is like Earth, but we have a larger sun. Our atmosphere is a similar combination of gases, but our planet is a third the size of Earth. Also, on Arcturus we have only one race and culture, whereas on Earth you have hundreds of different cultures and languages and races and religions. It's what makes Earth so wonderful, and what makes it so difficult for the planet to transition to the Fifth Dimension. With so many different viewpoints and contrasting opinions, it is challenging to function as a united planet." She has wound her braid into a bun and secured it by skewering it with a polished stick.

"Earthlings in general are not aware of life existing on other planets, so there's been no focus on acting as one unit on the planet." Her amber eyes meet mine, and she smiles.

"Arcturians are not human, but we are humanoid with many human characteristics. Our race is very tall and thin. We do not have a well-developed musculature because it isn't needed given our ability to control our environment with our thoughts."

"Like when Zeke levitated the stone," I say.

"Yes, it is the same," she says. "We also use telepathy to communicate with the spirit of our planet, enabling us to live in harmony with her. Consciousness, combined with technology, is the next evolution of man on Earth. Elevated consciousness is required to ascend to the Fifth Dimension."

It doesn't feel real that I'm on another planet, in another part of the galaxy, far away from Earth. This experience should make me feel different, somehow changed and elevated, but I feel only amazement. I have no sense of personal transformation. I desperately want to open up and have a transformative experience. If this doesn't do it, what will?

"In the Fifth Dimension there is no need for money, as we are able to manifest all of our needs using our thoughts. There is no crime or competition. Everyone is focused on personal growth and interpersonal relationships."

It sounds too good to be true. How can Earth and humanity ever get from where we are now to this peaceful, idyllic existence?

"We have no need of many of your technological devices because of our mastery of thought energy," Lorraine continues. "It frees us up to work on more creative or intellectual pursuits. We do, however, have powerful computers that we interact with to power our ships and enhance our healing methodologies. You would refer to these computers as artificial intelligence. There are strong protections in place to prevent AI machines from becoming independent of us and taking over."

I've been observing a group nearby on the lake shore. While I watch, one of them vanishes and an orb of light appears in her place. There are many orbs interspersed among the beings gathered.

"What are the orbs of light? I ask. "I saw them at the library too."

"Ah, you've noticed the higher dimensional ability to take a pure energy form," Zeke says. "Many beings, like Sophestus and Ariana, who you met on the *Athena*, have evolved to the point that they no longer need a physical body. As we progress through the dimensions, our presence in the physical world diminishes."

We stay on the shore of the Crystal Lake talking and basking in the energy from the crystal. It could be several minutes or several hours that pass. Time, or what I remember as time, has ceased to exist.

"THIS IS WHERE I leave you and send you back to Earth," Chief White Eagle says. "You will feel the crystal's energy healing power for several days, and the benefits can last for weeks. Remember that you can return to the Crystal Lake in your meditations whenever you wish."

I find this reassuring.

In turn, he places his palm on each of our foreheads and chants, "Elohim in the highest. Keep you in the Omega light." The last thing I hear before I enter the vortex of time and space is him calling, "Hey-ho!" and the *rum, bum, bum* of his drum.

23

WE'VE JUST FINISHED for the day at the dig on Wednesday afternoon, and I'm walking with my mom back to the dorms from the site. The last couple of days my thoughts have been filled with what happened on the *Athena* and Arcturus. As mind-blowing as it was to actually meet Ascended Masters and Star Beings, we're all still trying to come to terms with what it means for us to be Light Workers bringing the message of hope to Earth and her inhabitants.

But that is what I feel: hopeful. I'm hopeful because these Fifth Dimensional beings exist and want to help us. I'm hopeful that we can heal Earth and move in a positive direction. I'm not sure that Renee and Leo are fully on board with all of it, but Eric seems ready to move forward. I don't know what that means exactly, but I'm OK with letting it all unfold. I feel like a puzzle piece that was absent from my life has been slotted into place. The sense of something missing and the vague anxiety I felt before is gone, replaced with anticipation and a burgeoning joy.

My mom and I arrive in the clearing just as four vehicles pull into the parking area. Two are military SUVs in a drab green and two are black sedans with darkly tinted windows. Four men dressed in military uniforms and carrying what look like machine guns jump out of the SUVs, and four men in dark suits emerge from the sedans. One of them is Leo's dad.

My mom recognizes Mr. Stamatakis and confronts him directly. "What is this all about?" She gestures to the guns. "Guns are not allowed on university property. How dare you bring them to my dig site? You must leave immediately."

"I'm sorry, but we're here on government business. We have reason to believe two of your graduate students participated in recent domestic terrorist activities including the sabotage of a fracking well. They are fugitives from the law." Mr. Stamatakis calmly adjusts the cuffs of his dress shirt.

"You must be mistaken. All of the instructors go through a rigorous and thorough background check before they're hired on. Who are you referring to?" my mom says.

A small crowd of students has gathered around to watch. Leo and Eric stand beside me. Renee joins us when she arrives.

"They are the two graduate students we ate dinner with when I was here last. Zeke Waterson and Lorraine Tressler are the names they're using now. Your background check couldn't have been too thorough, because prior to five years ago there is virtually nothing on record about them. It's like they didn't exist before then."

My euphoria dims. How could I have been so naïve as to think that it would be easy to share the message of hope? Obviously there will be a lot of resistance. *And danger*, I think as I eye the exposed firepower.

But I'm ready. Maybe this is what it means to be a Spirit Warrior. *Bring it.*

I look over at Leo. His expression looks as alarmed as I feel. I don't think he knew anything about this. I'm about to go looking for Zeke and Lorraine to tell them to hide somewhere when I see them approaching the assembled group along the path.

"Here they come now." Mr. Stamatakis signals to one of the armed men to intercept them.

"What's going on?" Zeke asks in his usual friendly tone.

I move to stand between them and the army man. "This is ridiculous!" I exclaim. "They're not terrorists."

Leo comes up beside me. "What are you doing? Are you crazy?" He puts his hand on my elbow to pull me away, but I resist.

"Don't worry. Everything will be fine." Zeke says to me quietly. He tries to move me to one side, but I don't budge.

"These people seem to think you're terrorists," my mom says to Zeke and Lorraine. To Mr. Stamatakis, she says, "I thought you were with the Department of Energy, not the FBI or local law enforcement. You can't arrest them."

"We're with the FBI," one of the other men in suits says, and they all three pull out badges.

The clichéd picture they make—three federal agents in suits with badges—would be funny if it wasn't so deadly serious. All they need is dark glasses to complete the picture.

"You two are under arrest for suspicion of terrorist activities. We're going to take you in for questioning." Two of the FBI agents pull out sets of handcuffs and approach Zeke and Lorraine.

"No!" I burst out, hysteria rising in my throat. "You can't arrest them." I stretch out my arms as though I can somehow shield Zeke and Lorraine from harm and try to shove the nearest agent away.

"Young lady, it would be best if you would move out of the way," the agent says. The sidearm tucked under his jacket is visible when he raises his arm.

"It's OK, Marcie," Lorraine says. "We'll go with them to answer questions."

"What evidence do you have against them?" Now my mom has moved in front of Zeke and Lorraine as well.

"We discovered highly sophisticated military and technical data stored on a crystal belonging to them."

A memory comes flooding back to me: Leo breaking off the crystal in the underground cave.

"You . . . did this?" The shock I feel is like a dagger to my heart. "I remember now. I saw you break off a piece of crystal from the cave and shove it in your pocket. How could you? After what we saw!"

"I . . . I didn't know this would happen," Leo stammers. "I just thought I would share some of the knowledge stored in the crystal." He turns to his dad. "You never said anything about arresting them."

"Son, this has become bigger than just you and me. The data stored on this crystal is highly advanced, way beyond our own technology, and poses a threat to our national security. I have no choice but to take them in—for all the other reasons you shared with me as well," Mr. Stamatakis adds with a meaningful nod to Leo.

He apparently knows they're extraterrestrials too. That goes a long way to explaining why all these men with firepower are here.

I'm still trying to block the agents from handcuffing Zeke and Lorraine. I've positioned myself between them and the agents. "You can't just take them away. Don't they have rights?"

The agent pulls aside his jacket, displaying his handgun. "You need to move away right now, young lady, and let us do our job, and no one will get hurt."

"Are you actually threatening me with a gun?" I say, incredulous.

Leo yanks me back to stand next to him and the others, and this time I don't resist. The anger slowly drains out of me and is replaced by fear. What will they do to Zeke and Lorraine if they know that they are extraterrestrials? I imagine all sorts of gruesome tests and shudder.

"Put them in one of the jeeps," Mr. Stamatakis orders the FBI agents.

"I thought you were with the Department of Energy, not the FBI," I say.

Mr. Stamatakis looks at me as though considering what to say. "I have many responsibilities," is his cryptic reply.

Is he part of the shadow government Zeke referred to?

Two of the army guys come up, cuff Zeke and Lorraine, and escort them to the nearest jeep. I'm surprised that they go so willingly.

"We also need to bring in four of the students for questioning to find out what they know," Leo's dad says.

"What? No, I'm sorry, but I can't permit that. I'm their guardian while they are on site, and I won't agree to it." My mom is using her college professor I'm-in-charge-here voice, but it has little effect on Mr. Stamatakis.

"As I understand it most of the students are of legal age, and really the law is on our side here. I can take them in for questioning with or without your cooperation. You're welcome to accompany them if you wish."

I can't believe this is happening. It's all Leo's fault. It was wrong to include him. I was wrong to hope he would come around. He still has his hand on my arm. I wrench it free and take a step away from him. Warring emotions cross his face. He surprises me by confronting his dad.

"Why are you doing this?" His voice is taut with emotion. "I told you why they're here, to help us. They're not terrorists. What's with the military and FBI and the guns? I trusted you." He strides over to where his dad is standing and points a finger at his chest. "How can I trust you ever again?"

Mr. Stamatakis wraps his hand around Leo's finger. "I told you, this is bigger than just you and your friends and me and my department. The information you shared is a game changer. You have to understand that I had no choice. You're a hero, son, for bringing this forward."

I whisper something to Renee, and she passes it on to Eric. We lock eyes, and they nod. We're in agreement that we won't share the information that Zeke and Lorraine are extraterrestrials. Hopefully we can keep the rest of our stories similar enough to be believable.

They load us into a jeep and into one of the sedans. My mom's in the car with me. Immediately she's on the phone with my dad telling him what's happening and asking him to see if Mr. Clement can use his connections to get help. I'm scared about being questioned by the FBI, but I'm more worried about Zeke and Lorraine and what's in store for them.

When we get to town, the cars pull up in front of the ornately carved old county courthouse in the town center. It's built of Indiana limestone and must be over a hundred years old. There's a military helicopter on the lawn, and Zeke and Lorraine are being ushered into it by the army guys with the machine guns. One of the federal agents has his hands on their backs to keep their heads away from the rotating blades. Mr. Stamatakis gets on the helicopter too. I guess they're being taken somewhere else for questioning. I'm having a hard time believing this is happening. I thought Zeke and Lorraine would have more ability to control situations like this. I'm not sure what to think at this point.

The four of us are led into the courthouse and each put into a separate room. Even Leo is being questioned. I try the door and find it's locked, as I suspected it would be. It feels like about an hour goes by, and still no one has come for me. Time is measured in milliseconds as I wait. Finally, one of the FBI men enters the room.

"Can I use the bathroom?" I ask him.

"Umm, yes. I'll accompany you and wait outside." OK, kind of creepy. It's not like I'm planning to escape.

When we get back to the room, he starts asking questions about how long I've known Zeke and Lorraine, about what types of things they told us, and about what we may have done with them. He knows about the trip we took to Grand Caverns and the meditation we did on Emerald Mound. I answer as truthfully as possible without mentioning Zeke levitating stones or the visit to the *Athena* or Arcturus. The interrogation, if you could call it that, is pretty straightforward. But then he starts to get more aggressive.

"Did you go to a crystal cave while you were at Grand Caverns?" he asks.

"Yes." I figure the briefer and more truthful my answers are the better.

"How did you get there?"

"We walked."

"Your friends say that you were somehow transported to the cave. Isn't that how you got there?"

I figure the only person who would have shared that information is Leo, so I stick to my story and feign ignorance.

"I don't know what you mean by 'transported.'"

"Isn't it true that you also traveled to a spaceship with the two counselors and met beings from other planets?" He drums his fingers on the table and leans forward. "That, in fact, your counselors claim to be extraterrestrials, and have demonstrated abilities beyond our current technology?" His voice becomes more forceful and demanding.

My palms are sweating, and my heart is pounding so much in my chest that he must be able to hear it, but I stick to my story.

"That's absurd," I say. "They're just our graduate assistants at the dig. They taught us some meditation techniques, but that's it. I don't know anything about a spaceship. We just went on a sightseeing trip to Grand Caverns."

"Young lady, I hope you understand that by withholding information from us, you are violating the law and potentially putting your country at risk." He shakes his pen in my face. "If those two are indeed extraterrestrials, we need to know their intentions and capabilities so we can determine what to do with them."

Do with them? This confirms my concerns for Zeke and Lorraine. What will happen to them? My imagination is running wild.

"I've already told you everything I know." I'm sitting on my hands now to keep them from visibly shaking. "Why would two extraterrestrials be hanging out at a college archeological dig anyway? I told you before, this is absurd."

"You can cooperate and make this easy, or we can do this the hard way and be here for a long time—until you tell me what you know." He leans back in his chair. "I've got nothing but time."

I try to swallow, but my throat is dry. "Could I have some water, please?"

"Sure, whatever you want. Just tell me what you know." He leaves the room briefly and comes back with a bottle of water. "I'll give you the water when you tell me what you know."

He sets the bottle on the wooden table, taunting me. It's dripping with condensation, so it must be very cold. My tongue is sticking to the roof of my mouth. A growing fear starts creeping up from the base of my spine. How long can he keep us here? And where is my mom?

He continues to question me for what feels like another hour. He has me go through all the things we did with Zeke and Lorraine where something unusual happened. He seems to know what to ask already, as though he is just trying to get additional corroborating evidence from me.

My legs ache from sitting so long on the hard, wooden chair, and my nerves are frayed. The water bottle sits enticingly on the table in front of me. In the middle of this questioning, there's a knock at the door.

One of the other FBI agents pokes his head in. "We're done here."

"OK." The agent questioning me rises and pushes back his chair. He closes the portfolio where he'd been taking notes on our conversation and holds out his hand to me.

"Miss Horton, I'll take my leave of you now, but be prepared to be called back for additional questioning."

I let his hand hang in the air. There's no way I'm going to shake his hand. I don't say anything; there really isn't anything to say.

"You're free to go," the other agent tells me.

I grab the water bottle and unscrew the cap.

He puts a restraining hand on my arm. "This investigation is highly sensitive, and you are not to discuss it with anyone." He raises his eyebrows for emphasis. "Do I make myself clear?"

I nod and guzzle the now tepid water as I follow them to the hallway. Eric is already there with my mom. I'm close to tears in reaction to the whole ordeal.

My mom gives me a big hug, then holds me at arms' length. "Are you OK?"

"Yeah, just exhausted from all of this. Can we get out of here?"

"Good idea. I think I saw some benches on the front lawn where we can wait for the others."

Night fell while we were being questioned. I welcome the enveloping darkness. It makes me feel hidden from our interrogators. I sit down gratefully on one of the benches.

Eric sits beside me. "Did they just ask you the same things over and over again?"

I nod.

"Did you tell them anything?"

I shake my head. "No."

"Me neither, but it wasn't always easy. They seemed to have a lot of information already, probably courtesy of Leo."

"That's what I thought too. Did you see them take Zeke and Lorraine away in a helicopter? Where do you think they're taking them? I'm really worried."

"Mom's been talking to Mr. Clement on the phone. She got in touch with some of his contacts who may have helped get us out of there, but I'm not sure if they'll have any pull with Zeke and Lorraine. The FBI is going with the story that they are suspected terrorists and dangerous. It's all extremely hush-hush." He rubs his hands against his shorts as if scrubbing off the taint of the FBI agents.

Leo walks down the steps toward us with his eyes downcast. Renee follows behind him. He won't make eye contact. I'm taken off guard by the surge of anger I feel toward him and decide ignoring him is the best policy for the moment. I can confront him later.

"How're we going to get back?" I ask my mom.

She's just gotten off her phone. "Professor Fraser is coming to get us in the university van. I'm sorry we couldn't get all of you out of there sooner. Mr. Clement's contacts came up against a lot of opposition to releasing you." She looks at me shrewdly. "I'd like some answers of my own. There's more to the excursions you took with Zeke and Lorraine than you're telling. You can fill me in on the way back."

I'm not sure how much I should tell her. It's one thing to lie to the federal government and quite another to lie to your mom.

Since we never got any dinner, we stop to eat at one of those twenty-four-hour restaurants on the way home. It's after ten o'clock, and we're hungry. It seems as though everyone had a similar experience to me: lots of questions about what we did with Zeke and Lorraine and about what they showed us. Everyone kept to the basic information about hikes and meditations and said nothing unusual about Grand Caverns.

"So what's the truth?" My mom points at us with the french fry she's holding. "What didn't you tell them about Zeke and Lorraine?"

I glance at the others and feel like I've been designated as the spokesperson since she's my mom. She's Eric's mom, too, but he gives me the nod to proceed.

"You may not believe me if I tell you."

"Try me."

"OK." I plunge ahead. "Zeke and Lorraine are Star Beings from the planet Arcturus in the Arcturus star system. They're here to help stop humans from destroying the Earth and to help us to ascend to the Fifth Dimension. They took us to their spaceship in the corridor between Jupiter and Mars where there are dozens of cloaked spaceships from other planets. They also showed us what their planet, Arcturus, is like." I pause and look at my mom.

She's very still and has stopped eating her french fries, but she doesn't say anything.

"They came to show us how to teach others about taking care of our planet and how to ascend to the Fifth Dimension. We're supposed to be catalysts who help people who are looking for answers." I'm gripping the edge of the tabletop anticipating her reaction.

"Whoa. That is *not* the answer I was expecting. You can't be serious," my mom replies. She looks at the others. "Is this what you all believe happened?"

They nod in agreement.

"Yeah, it really happened. Zeke even levitated a block of stone as big as a compact car," Eric says. "He healed Mr. Kuhn at the fracking meeting."

"Wow, extraterrestrials." She's quiet for a moment. "It's a lot to take in. I can certainly believe the part about humans destroying the planet. But traveling to a spaceship, and dozens of spaceships hanging out in our solar system? That's harder to believe." She wipes her hands on a napkin.

Eric and Renee start talking, and together we tell her and Dr. Fraser everything that's happened with Zeke and Lorraine. We tell them about Greystone Mountain, Emerald Mound, and Grand Caverns and about the *Athena* and Arcturus.

"I didn't want to be part of this mission, whatever it is, at all." Renee is alternately pleating and unfolding the hem of her shirt. "But I'm starting to see how important it is. I feel like it's a responsibility I can't shirk. Frightened or not." She grasps Eric's hand.

Leo hasn't said anything. His head is bowed down and he's not meeting our eyes.

"I don't blame you," my mom says. "If federal agents are involved, it does seem somewhat frightening. I'm not entirely convinced about any of this, I have to say."

"I guess you could say that this is the start of our mission—telling you about it. We already know you're against fracking and other ways that we're harming the Earth. I guess it's the whole Star Being part that's a stretch," I say.

My mom sits back in the large booth where we're seated in a circle. "What do you think, Simon?" she asks Dr. Fraser.

"I don't know what to believe." He shakes his head.

"Well, at the very least, I can accept that all of you believe Zeke and Lorraine are from another planet, even given how far out that seems. Your father and I have always believed in the existence of extraterrestrials, or Star Beings, in theory. The real thing is altogether an entirely different matter." She lets out a little laugh. "I would have loved to talk to them about it myself. Maybe someday, if as you say they plan to reveal themselves to the world in the future."

"What do you think will happen to them?" I ask.

"I have no idea, but probably nothing good. I imagine they'll be tested and questioned extensively. How did the FBI find out about them anyway?"

We all look at Leo.

"I told my dad about them." He speaks for the first time, his voice coming out in a croak. He looks up, and his face is so stricken that my heart softens a little. "He's involved in some very secret government activities, and he's mentioned ETs before.

I didn't think they would arrest them and take them away or question all of us for hours."

"What did you think they would do, ask them to tea?" Eric says.

"You're telling your mom now, aren't you?" he says. "I thought I was helping. I know I haven't been completely on board with what Zeke and Lorraine are doing, but after tonight, that's all changed." He swipes a hand over his eyes. "I'm sorry for what happened tonight. I honestly didn't know my dad would do this. I was confused about who was doing the right thing . . . I mean, he's my dad after all . . . but now I know. I'm so sorry."

"You didn't help Zeke and Lorraine by telling your dad. And my mom doesn't work for the government on some secret assignments involving ETs," I say.

"I know. I let them down," he says.

"You let all of us down," I say. *Especially me.*

My mom reaches over and pats his hand. "Maybe it will be all right. Maybe our government will treat them properly."

"Are you kidding?" Eric barks out. "That's not likely."

"Zeke did tell me not to worry, that everything would be OK, so maybe it will be. I don't really know what to think." I'm holding on to whatever hope I can.

We finish our food and climb back into the van for the ride home. I'm surprised when Leo sits down beside me. I scoot over and make room for him. He reaches out to hold my hand, and I let him take it in his, but my simmering anger overrides the usual pleasure I get at his touch. He meets my gaze and doesn't look away.

"Can you forgive me?" His dark eyes are red rimmed and full of sadness. "You have every right to be mad at me. I made a mistake. A terrible mistake." He rubs the back of his neck with his free hand.

"I don't know," I say truthfully, letting the anger show in my voice. "Maybe you're not who I thought you were. I've always known we had different beliefs, and maybe I naïvely hoped that you might change to my point of view, but I never imagined you'd betray us. You broke my trust in you, and I'm not sure it can be repaired." I pull my hand away from his and hold his gaze.

His eyes are pleading, and part of me wants to forgive him, but I can't. Not yet. The pain of betrayal is too raw. My anger protects me from being devastated, so I wrap it around me like a cloak.

"I need more time," I tell him.

"Thank you," he says. "That's more than I'd hoped for."

I fall asleep on the way home. When I wake up, I find my head is resting on Leo's shoulder. I snuggle closer into his side before it all comes flooding back.

I move away from him and straighten my clothes. Zeke and Lorraine have been arrested and taken away to be questioned, either as terrorists or ETs. I don't know which is worse.

24

LIFE AT THE dig goes on as before. Our group is broken up and reassigned to the other teams headed by the remaining grad students. After all the excitement of our experiences with Zeke and Lorraine and traveling to outer space, it's a big letdown to be back in the regular everyday world. On top of that, we have no idea what's happening to them or if they're OK.

I can't help feeling like they abandoned us. Even though they were the ones taken away in handcuffs, I'm pretty sure they could have resisted, or vanished, or *something*. As it is, they left us wondering what fate is in store for them and with no idea what we're supposed to do without their guidance.

Leo and I are assigned to the same new team, but I try my best to avoid him. I'm not ready to go back to the way things were between us. Maybe he didn't anticipate what would happen, but he still broke my trust. I'm just not sure about our relationship anymore.

I'm working in my section excavating with my trowel when I get a sense of *knowing* about Zeke and Lorraine. They're all right. They've escaped. I'm sure of it. Relief washes over me, and I sit back on my haunches to steady myself.

They're OK.

I hadn't realized how tense and afraid I'd been. I'm almost giddy with the release of emotions. I close my eyes and hug my knees to my chest.

Someone taps me on the shoulder, and I open my eyes to see Leo. The cause of my distress.

"What do you want?" I ask. It comes out harsher than I intended.

He crouches down next to me. "I need to talk to you." He looks around us. "Privately."

"OK." I gesture over to the road that runs next to the dig site. "There's no one over there."

I don't really have it in me to be mean to Leo, even given what he did. He's obviously suffering for it, as we've all be treating him like a pariah. And now that I know Zeke and Lorraine are OK, I am more able to be generous in dealing with him.

I undo my bandana from around my neck and take off my hat to wipe the sweat from my forehead. "What is it?"

"I have good news to tell you," he begins.

"Zeke and Lorraine escaped," I interrupt.

"Yeah," he says, surprised. "I got a text from my dad. They disappeared from the cells where they were being held. But it *just* happened. He contacted me in case they turn up here." He tilts his head to one side and squints at me. "How did you know?"

"I got a message too," I say. "But not on my phone." The tone of my voice dares him to question me, but he doesn't. "I hope you're not planning to tell your dad anything." I give him a sharp look.

"Don't worry. If they do show up here, I won't be telling anyone," he says quickly. "There was no sign of the locks on their cells being tampered with, and the security cameras show them simply vanishing into thin air."

"Yes!" I pump my fist in the air. "They must have teleported or shimmered back to the *Athena*. I should have known they could. We'll have to tell the others. Maybe they'll turn up here and let us know they're OK and tell us what to do next."

But they don't come back. We're all waiting and hoping to see them again, because everything feels unfinished. We have so many unanswered questions since we came back from the *Athena* and Arcturus, and I, for one, want more direction on what to do with my burgeoning ability to connect to the Field. Just teaching people about raising their vibrations and meditating more doesn't feel significant. Maybe Zeke and Lorraine can't risk coming back, but they left things unfinished. None of us knows how to move forward without them.

After we finish at the dig site one afternoon, I take a walk through the woods to the bench beside the river. For a while I sit and watch the water flow past. It's calming and a bit meditative. By my feet there's a little pile of rocks. I wonder if I can levitate them. They're not very big, and no one's here to see me. When I moved the rock in the cave it was under extreme duress, and Zeke helped me, and he also helped me by the stream before. Can I do it on my own?

I move from the bench to the grass in front of the pile, facing the river and resting my hands on my knees with my palms facing up. I calm my breathing and center my thoughts on the stones. With my eyes closed, I imagine the stones lifting off the ground to hover in the air. It feels like a gossamer thread, as fragile as a spider's web, leads from my heart to where the stones lie. I'm not sure if it's working, and I hesitate to open my eyes for fear of breaking my concentration.

The snap of a branch startles me. My eyes fly open. Before me, the rocks hover in the air.

"Marcie?"

I whip my head around and see Leo coming out of the trees. The rocks thump to the ground behind me.

"What are you doing here?"

"I saw you go into the woods, and I followed. I was hoping I could talk to you alone. Were you meditating? I didn't mean to interrupt you." He runs his hand through his hair and ducks his head.

I can't help the way my heart beats faster when he does that. I smother those feelings with my anger.

"Yes, I was meditating." I don't think he saw the stones. Even if my body says otherwise, I'm not pleased to see him. I want to practice levitating.

"Can I sit down?" he asks.

"Yeah, OK." He either doesn't hear the coolness of my tone or doesn't want to hear it, because he comes and sits beside me.

He plucks blades of grass with his long, brown fingers. I wait for him to speak.

"I wanted to tell you I'm sorry again. I wasn't trying to hide anything from you. I was just sharing stuff with my dad. The things happening around Zeke and Lorraine were amazing, and I told him about it. They never said to keep anything a secret."

"What about the crystal? You kept *that* a secret. I saw you put it in your pocket."

"That's true." He draws a deep breath and exhales slowly. "But I had no idea my dad would come with guns and the FBI. You have to believe me. I really didn't know." He turns his head to look at me and his eyes are pleading.

It would be easy to continue to blame Leo for what happened, but it's not his fault. It's fear and the drive for power and control that created his dad and people like him. They have their own agenda, and it's one of the reasons Zeke and Lorraine came to help us. I can forgive Leo, but I'm not sure if I can give him my trust. His betrayal cut me deeply, and I'm not prepared to be hurt again.

"I believe you," I say.

He visibly relaxes.

I pick up one of the stones and roll it between my fingers. "I know you didn't want any harm to come to us, or to Zeke and Lorraine. But now they're gone, and I feel like it's unfinished. It can't have ended like that."

"I'm sorry. Maybe they'll come back."

"How can they, when they're wanted by the FBI? Now they're escaped fugitives on top of everything else."

"I think they could contact us if they . . . " He lets his voice trail off.

"Wanted to." I finish the sentence for him. "That's the thing. As more time passes, it feels more and more like they don't want to."

We sit in silence for several minutes. Just being near him makes my heart happy, but my mind is uncertain. Finally, he asks the question I've been dreading.

"Soooo what about us? You and me, I mean." He won't look me in the eye.

I reach out and place my hand on his arm. He looks up at me, his expression hopeful.

"I really like you, Leo." I swallow the lump in my throat. "But things have changed. I don't think I can go back to the way things were before."

Now his expression is stricken. Is this what I really want? Am I doing the right thing?

"Is it because of what I think about fracking, and my not being as accepting of Zeke and Lorraine as you?"

"Basically, yes. We have very different outlooks on the world." I sit up straighter and square my shoulders, pulling my protective cloak of anger around me, holding my pain inside. "What you did hurt me too. You didn't just betray Zeke and Lorraine, you betrayed me."

"I know, and I'm so sorry. But I've changed!" He takes my hands in both of his. "I've realized that the government and big energy companies have been lying to us all along. My dad has been too." He says the last sadly. "I didn't believe what Zeke and Lorraine told us at first, but when we visited their spaceship, that changed me. I get it now. I know they came to help us." He places a fingertip on my cheek and meets my eyes, his gaze intense. "Please. Please give me a chance to show you that I've changed . . . and how much I really care about you. I didn't mean to hurt you."

"I'm sorry." I pull away. "I can't." His shoulders slump.

"OK. I won't bother you anymore. I wish none of this had ever happened." He gets up and walks toward the woods. Right before he starts on the path, he looks back at me, his expression unspeakably sad.

Once I'm sure he's out of earshot, I let the tears flow.

WHILE WE'VE BEEN preoccupied with federal agents and extraterrestrials, United Oil has made significant progress on its fracking activities in the area. According to my dad, several property owners signed up immediately and will allow expanded fracking on their existing wells. United Oil wasted no time in getting production underway, and there are already at least two fully active fracking wells on the neighboring farmland.

A little while before dinner, I'm playing cards in the shelter with Scott, Lainey, and Nora. I feel almost normal with them since they don't know the truth about Zeke and Lorraine, but Lainey brings them up.

"Does anyone know what happened with Zeke and Lorraine?" she asks. "Someone said they were taken away in handcuffs."

"Yeah, I heard that too." Nora draws a card, looks at it for a second, then discards it.

"No one knows what happened to them," I can say honestly. "The FBI said they were terrorists." I take a card from the deck. It's a three. I play it on the threes already down.

"No way. That can't be true," Scott says. "They were totally cool. What did the FBI say they did?"

"Supposedly they interfered with one of the fracking wells. Sabotage or something. Which is ridiculous." This gives me an idea, though.

"Hey, why don't we organize a demonstration at one of the fracking wells? Not anything like sabotage, but I bet we could get some of the dig students to participate, and maybe even some of the locals."

"That's a great idea." Scott lays down a straight and throws up his hands. "Out!"

"Noooo!" Lainey pouts at Scott. "I needed that five."

"Sorry. I got it first." He grins and winks at her.

Some obvious chemistry is going on there. I'm glad for Lainey, but my mind is already whirring with plans for the antifracking demonstration.

He turns his attention back to me. "They'll have a crew there 24/7 to keep the well running full tilt, so we could have it this Saturday."

"OK, I'll start spreading the word." The dinner bell sounds, and I push back from the table ready to get started.

That evening and the next day I spread the word about the demonstration on Saturday. We make signs to bring with us, and I ask my dad to contact the locals who are opposed to fracking. Most of the field study students and grad students want to join in, and of course Eric and Renee do as well, but my mom is far from on board.

"I'm not sure a demonstration is such a good idea, honey," she says. "You don't want to fan the fires of animosity that are already burning. Remember what happened at the coffee shop? And at Nana and Pops's house?"

We're sitting on the porch swing of the old farmhouse. Crickets and cicadas fill the air around us with a symphony of chips, whirrs, and hums.

"I just want to be moving forward with something, you know? Something that will make a difference. I don't want to feel powerless against big corporations or the government anymore. Having a demonstration is a small thing, but at least we'll be taking action," I say. "Nothing bad will happen. You'll see."

25

A GOOD-SIZED GROUP turns out for our demonstration—about thirty people, ten locals and twenty students. We're walking back and forth with our signs about fifty yards from the fence surrounding the well pad. At first we were chanting antifracking slogans, but we're taking a break from that now. The United Energy workers are basically ignoring us, and no one else is around to notice what we're doing. I notified the local news agencies that we'd be out here, and I'm hoping they arrive soon, before people start to leave. The more demonstrators we have when they get here, the better.

A truck pulls off the main road onto the access road and stops next to where we're demonstrating. A man and woman get out and come toward us. Since I organized the protest, I'm the de facto leader of our group, so I walk over to meet them.

"Hi, I'm Marcie Horton." I extend my hand. "Are you here to join the protest?"

"Yes, as a matter of fact, we are." The woman grasps my hand in hers and shakes it vigorously. "We're from Earth Cause. Mr. Clements works with us. I'm Becky, and this is Ron." She's small and round and he's tall and thin. They remind me of the Jack Sprat nursery rhyme. I shake his hand too.

"Oh, that's great!" I tell them. "Welcome. We're so glad you're here. We've already been out a couple of hours, and I'm hoping the TV news station gets here before people start leaving. Maybe you could talk to the media when they arrive."

"Absolutely," she says. "We have pretty good momentum going in gaining opposition to fracking in the area, and any news coverage helps a lot."

"Really? You're making progress? That's good news."

I lead them over to the group and make introductions. When I get to Leo, I'm a little uncomfortable, but he greets them warmly and even smiles at me, although his eyes are sad.

We haven't spoken since that day by the river, and I was surprised he came to the demonstration. I don't really know what to say to him. It's not like we can be friends. I've caught him looking at me when I've risked a glace in his direction, but he's kept his word and left me alone. I'm still trying to sort out how I feel. It's a mixture of hurt, betrayal, and attraction. I can't deny that I'm still drawn to him, but is that enough to outweigh everything else?

The Earth Cause people start talking with a small group of demonstrators. The group gradually grows as the others form a semicircle around them until everyone who came to the demonstration is listening. They're basically giving us a pep talk, telling us that what we're doing matters and not to get discouraged. They've been talking for about ten minutes when a TV news van pulls up behind their truck.

I recognize the news anchor from local TV when she gets out of the van followed by her cameraman. She changes from pumps into flats for the trek across the soft ground.

"Hi, I'm Stacy Murray from WTTW News 8 in Evansville. We'd like to interview you about the antifracking protest for tonight's six o'clock news. Who's in charge?" She looks around. She's holding a microphone in her hand, but she's not speaking into it.

"Marcie's in charge." Lainey pushes me forward. "She organized the protest."

"Yes, I—I'm Marcie Horton," I stammer. Then I square my shoulders. "I'd be happy to answer some questions. We also have representatives here from Earth Cause." I indicate Becky and Ron.

"Perfect," she says. "I'm going to do a brief introduction, then we'll move to the interview." She turns to her cameraman. "OK, I'm ready. Cue me in."

A red light on the camera starts flashing. He counts down with his fingers in the air—one, two, three—and points to Ms. Murray, signaling her to begin.

"We're here at one of the first full-scale fracking sites in southern Indiana. You can see behind me the drill rig, tankers, and equipment for the operation. Fracking for natural gas has been touted as a way to extract 'clean energy' that is abundant in the US. Supporters also say fracking will help us to rely less heavily on Middle Eastern oil." She speaks directly to the camera, the light trained on her.

"But not everyone is in favor of fracking. I'm here with a protest group, and we're also joined by representatives from Earth Cause, an organization that opposes fracking." She turns to me. "This is Marcie Horton with the group demonstrating. Marcie, please tell our viewers why you oppose fracking when it could be a solution to our energy needs." She holds the microphone under my chin.

Out of the corner of my eye, I see another van pull up behind the Earth Cause van. The United Energy logo is emblazoned on its side. Irritated, I pull my attention back to Stacy Murray. I want to answer her questions before they get here and try to contradict me.

"Well, first of all, natural gas is not clean energy when compared to wind, solar, and hydro energy. Burning natural gas still releases CO_2 into our atmosphere and contributes to greenhouse gases, resulting in climate change." My words come out in a rush, so I try to slow down and gather my thoughts.

"The other issue is the damage that fracking itself causes. The chemicals pumped into the ground are totally unregulated, and many are known carcinogens. The chemicals poison our aquifers, and the methane gas released by fracking contaminates the well water used by residents to drink and bathe and to water their crops and livestock. Not to mention there's a link between fracking and increased earthquakes."

By this time, the now familiar Stuart Houseman has reached us with his cronies. I glare at them.

Stacy Murray briefly looks over at them and returns her attention to me. "So why would anyone want to allow fracking on their property?"

"The energy companies deny that there is anything harmful about fracking. Once the landowners start experiencing problems, it's too late," I say.

"Ms. Murray?" Stuart Houseman says in his oily voice. "I'm with United Energy, and I'd like the opportunity to address the claims asserted by Miss Horton."

The gleam in Ms. Murray's eyes is unmistakable. She turns her smile full throttle onto Mr. Houseman.

"Well, of course, I'm sure our viewers would love to hear the other side of the story." She moves the microphone away from me to Mr. Houseman.

He proceeds to give his spiel about fracking being safe and there being no evidence to the contrary. "If you'd like, I'll take you closer to the site and explain how everything works," he says.

"Yes, that would be great," Stacy answers.

They stop filming and turn toward the well site.

"By the way, young lady, you and your friends are trespassing. I could have you arrested." Mr. Houseman sneers as he passes me. "But you'd love that wouldn't you? Add more fuel to your cause."

I just glower at him.

Leo comes up alongside me. "I think I'll just follow them up there," he says. "No telling what that jerk will say."

"Uh, OK, um, thanks."

Maybe Leo *has* changed. He's here, isn't he? And actively doing something against United Energy. I watch him walk away, wondering. Ever since the United Energy guys arrived, I felt anxiety start raising its ugly head. Maybe it's because of Houseman crashing our protest, but I'm not entirely sure that's it.

Our demonstrators started chanting the antifracking slogans again when the news team arrived. They're still going strong. I pick up my sign and join them, but I keep my eye on Stacy Murray and Houseman. They stop just outside the fence near the fracking water tankers, the ones full of toxic chemicals. The camera is rolling, and Stacy moves the microphone between them. Leo stands off to the side, listening. At one point, he steps forward and says something to the camera. The reporter moves the microphone to him, and Houseman gets a thunderous look on his face, but masks it quickly.

KABOOM!

Without warning, a massive explosion rips through the well site with an ear-splitting roar. Flames shoot fifty feet in the air. Even as far away as we are, I feel the force of the blast. It knocks Leo and the others off their feet. They are dangerously close to the flames. Sirens start going off, adding to the chaos. Without making a conscious decision, I'm running toward them and the fire.

When I'm about thirty yards away, one of the tankers explodes, obscuring my view. I stop running and stare in horror at the flames. The four of them are surrounded by fire.

"Leo!" I scream. "Leo, can you hear me?" I know he can't hear me, but I can't help calling out to him. I try to move closer, but it's too hot.

Then he answers me. *Marcie? It's so hot. Can't breathe. Get back.* The words aren't spoken out loud; I hear them in my head. We're communicating telepathically.

Mere seconds have passed. What can I do? *Oh God, oh God, oh God!*

I try to calm down and think. The air is searing my lungs. There must be something I can do. A shield. Maybe I can create a shield like Zeke did in the cavern. I focus all my concentration on making a shield. The air ripples. I feel a strength and power course through me as I draw from the air around me. My energy body expands five, ten, twenty feet beyond my body. I'm vibrating faster and faster, pulsing rhythmically. An explosion of power comes from my very core. I am transformed. I am one with all things.

A thin line of blue shimmers around me. I did it. I created a shield. I run toward the flames, praying it will protect me and the others.

I hesitate only a moment when I reach the inferno. The heat from the fire is intense, but bearable. The flames don't reach me through the shield. I plunge in.

Orange, white, and red-hot light surrounds me. I can't see anything beyond the roiling tongues of flame. I move forward cautiously, not sure if I'm going in the right direction. Finally, I reach what I had hoped to find. A clearing. The four of them are standing in the center with their backs together, holding hands, the flames closing in around them. Leo sees me.

"Marcie! What are you doing? How did you get here?" His dark eyes are frightened and alarmed.

I reach for his hands, so emotional that I can hardly speak. How could I have shut him out? I don't even know why anymore. It's no longer important. I brush the thoughts aside. We have to move. Now.

"Hurry!" I shout over the din of the fire. "I created a shield. Get the others to stay close behind me. We'll walk out together."

I mentally extend the shield to cover the other three. They balk at first, but the shield is visible around us, and it's holding the flames at bay. Once again, I walk into a wall of fire.

Leo's holding on to my waist. I look back and see Stacy, Houseman, and the cameraman close behind him. I move slowly to ensure that we stay together. Tongues of fire lick the edges of the shimmering shield, but it holds. I'm concentrating fiercely, terrified that the shield will fail and we'll be burnt to a crisp. After several awful minutes, I step onto green grass and out of the fire. We keep moving until we're well away from it. I crumple to the ground, utterly spent.

"Marcie. Marcie!" I hear someone calling me from far away. Now they're shaking me. I just want to sleep. "Wake up! Marcie, can you hear me? Wake up!"

I try to open my eyes, but they're glued shut. When I finally pull the lids apart, I see Leo bending over me, his eyes streaming and bloodshot.

"Thank God," he says. "Are you OK? When you collapsed, I thought something had happened to you." He brushes his hand along my cheek.

"I'm OK. Just wiped out." I put my hands on either side of his face. "Oh, Leo, I'm so sorry." I bring his face down to mine and kiss him.

When we break apart, his face is alight and his eyes are shining. "I don't know what you have to be sorry about. You just saved my life, but if that's how you apologize, then I accept." He leans down to kiss me again. He tastes like smoke and salt and something that is just Leo.

I pull back to catch my breath. It's important that I finish what I have to say. "I should have believed you when you said you didn't know what would happen with Zeke and Lorraine. That you weren't betraying them—and me. And I can see that you've changed. I'm sorry."

"No, you were right. It was all my fault." He leans back and runs his hand over his face, his tone serious now. "If I'd been more open minded and accepting of them, none of it would have happened. If I hadn't told my dad what we were doing, Zeke and Lorraine would still be here."

He's overcome by a sudden coughing fit. When he gets his breathing under control, he wipes the tears streaming from his eyes and looks at me intently. "It's me who should be sorry. You were doing the right thing all along. I wasn't."

He brushes his fingertips along my face again and tucks my hair behind my ear. "Then you go and save my life. How did you do that? Did you connect with the Field?"

"Yes, I connected, and something happened. It changed me. No, that's not the right word. Enhanced. It enhanced me. It magnified my strengths and good qualities. I feel somehow more, if that even makes sense." I frown in frustration. "It's so hard to put into words. I was so terrified for you, for all four of you. I had to do something. I remembered Zeke's shield in the cavern, and I focused my mind, and it happened."

"Well, I'm beyond glad that you did. It was amazing. *You're* amazing. I know I haven't been very supportive of your abilities, but I'm totally on board now. You've made me a believer."

"I'm really glad." My lips curve into a smile. "They're not just my abilities, though. Anyone can do it if they focus and practice. You could do it too."

"I doubt it, but I'll take your word for it. You're more open to it."

"Maybe, but this time I think I did do it all by myself. I didn't sense Zeke and Lorraine helping me. I'm still not entirely sure how I did it, and I don't know if I can do it again when I'm not under duress, but it's a place to begin."

"That's for sure. A really good place.'"

Now I'm ready to set it aside, for the moment, at least. I have other things on my mind. "Can we leave the rest of it in the past and start over? I want to move forward."

"Definitely. I want that too." He leans his forehead against mine.

The fire trucks and ambulances start arriving. Several of the rig crew were badly burned and require immediate attention. Fortunately they were on the ground on the side away from the explosion, so no one was killed.

The paramedics treat Leo for smoke inhalation, but he doesn't want to go to the hospital. I see Stacy Murray being loaded into an ambulance on a stretcher. Her cameraman starts their van, turns it around, and drives away. I have a selfish hope that he'll get the news footage to the station in time for the six o'clock news. Stuart Houseman is off to the side being treated. He looks at me strangely, but I'm beyond caring. Let him think what he wants. I'm sure he doesn't want to talk about the explosion.

All I want to do now is get to my bed in the dorm and sleep for hours.

26

My hand is throbbing. I look down and see the pink crystal with the Sacred Triangle glowing softly in my hand, pulsing with an electrical current. It's dark. I'm standing alone at the base of Angel Mound where the circular path begins. I feel compelled to walk up the path. The closer I get to the top, the brighter the crystal glows, and the stronger I sense its electrical current. The Native spirits whisper encouragement to me as I climb, giving me the confidence that this is what I'm supposed to be doing.

When I reach the top, I come up short. Chief White Eagle stands at the center of the mound and Native spirits dance around him. He doesn't speak but bows his head to me. I watch the sinuous and flowing dance for several minutes, mesmerized. Then Chief White Eagle and the Natives vanish, leaving only a faint glow where he'd been standing.

I'm still groggy when I wake from the dream. I lie there for a moment and try to make sense of it. Chief White Eagle and the Native spirits seemed to be holding a ceremony. Is that what I'm supposed to do, bring the crystal to Angel Mound? I get up, rub the sleep out of my eyes, and take a long drink from the glass beside my bed to ease my rough throat. I need to find the others to tell them about the dream so we can figure out what to do next.

"WHEN SHOULD WE do this?" Leo asks after I fill in him, Eric, and Renee on the details of my dream.

We've gathered next to the stream behind the faculty dorm, where we know we won't be overheard.

"I'm not sure. Wait! Isn't the summer solstice coming up? That would be a good day to go," I say.

"It's on the twenty-first. Today's the nineteenth," Eric says. "So we go to the mound in two days, on Monday night."

"What exactly are we going to do?" Renee asks.

"Hopefully we'll know when we get there," I answer.

We have to wait until Monday to retrieve the pink crystal, as the trailer with the artifacts is locked up on the weekend. Since I wrote down the codes identifying where it is stored, I'm elected to retrieve it. Renee comes with me for moral support and to block the view of me rifling through the artifacts. Leo tags along at the last minute.

Just as I find the bag holding the crystal, someone from my new team starts coming toward the trailer. "Quick, we need a distraction," Renee says to Leo.

"OK." His eyes light up with a mischievous gleam. He wraps his arms around me and presses his lips against mine. My mouth is already open in shock, so he has no trouble probing my lips with his tongue. It's a total make-out kiss—right in front of the whole dig team.

"I got it," Renee says. "You can stop now."

"So soon?" Leo says. "I was really enjoying myself."

I extricate myself from his embrace. I'm a little embarrassed by the kiss, but I still can't stop myself smiling from ear to ear. I swat him on the shoulder. "Wasn't that a little much?"

"Not at all. And it effectively deterred anyone from coming to the trailer while Renee grabbed the artifact bag." He lowers his voice to a whisper. "I'm trying to make up for lost time."

I can't argue with that.

My two new team members start clapping slowly. One of them says, "Nice show." Leo bows slightly at the waist, and I blush what I know must be a deep crimson given how hot my face is. I can't get back to my section fast enough. At least it was worth the embarrassment. Renee got the crystal.

On the night of the solstice the four of us gather at the base of Angel Mound. I'm holding the crystal with the Sacred Triangle. Just as in my dream, it glows and pulses. Also as in my dream, the Native spirits are gathered around us, offering support and guidance. We silently move along the path to the summit of the mound. When we get to the top, we naturally form a circle, with one of us in each of the cardinal directions, north, south, east, and west.

"I think we should hold hands," Renee says.

"Yes." I place the crystal on the ground in the center of our circle, aligning it with where the sun is just now setting for the summer solstice. When the crystal touches the ground, I hear a low humming sound that comes from the mound and vibrates up through the soles of my feet.

"The mound is resonating at some frequency that's making it vibrate," Leo says. "Can you feel it?"

We all feel it. I also hear it as a low melody singing to my soul.

"I think we should shimmer to raise our vibration," Eric says.

I close my eyes and imagine myself ensconced in my cosmic egg. It hums and vibrates around me, pulsing faster and faster. When my vibration matches the frequency of the mound there is a resonance and melding of all our vibrations with the mound and one another. We're joined together harmonically like instruments in a song, creating the music and flowing with the sound.

A bright light erupts in the center of the circle, so bright that I can see through my closed eyelids. I open my eyes. Before me stand two illuminated beings. They are very tall, over seven feet, I would guess, and very slim. They're glowing with a golden halo all around them. It takes me a moment to realize that they're Zeke and Lorraine.

"You're all right! And you came back!" I want to run and hug them, but I don't want to break the circle.

They have the translucent skin of the Arcturians we saw on the *Athena* and by Crystal Lake, and their facial features are smaller than humans' in proportion to their size. Their eyes are large, though, and their hair is the same. Lorraine has her mane of golden hair and Zeke his dark, shoulder-length hair.

"Yes, we are here in our true Arcturian forms to help you with the final step. You must activate the energy of Angel Mound by unblocking its ley line. This process already began when you placed the sacred crystal in the center of your circle and aligned it with the ley line. You can feel the mound responding," Lorraine says.

"What will happen when we activate the mound and unblock the ley line?" Eric asks.

"Activating the energy of the mound and its ley line will connect them to Earth's energy grid. This will raise the vibration of Earth so she can repair the damage that's been done to her and prepare for ascension to the higher vibration of the Fifth Dimension."

At the fracking site, when I was able to create the shield, I had felt myself begin to change, becoming more than I was before. I have the same feeling now.

"But we're activating more than just the mound. We're activating ourselves," I say. "Isn't that right?"

"Yes, my child," Lorraine says. "This ceremony will serve to elevate all of your spiritual energies, bringing you closer to the Fifth Dimension. Although, Marcie, you began to be activated during the explosion at the fracking site. You called upon your own power and strength using Fifth Dimension energy to create the protective shield." I only nod in agreement. That experience had left me feeling like I'd been opened up to a new level. I'm ready now for what I came here to do in this lifetime, whatever that may be.

"You're so beautiful," Renee tells Zeke and Lorraine, and it's true. They were attractive as humans, but now they're larger than life, glowing with health and wellness and an inner beauty. They move in a sinuous rhythm that's almost like dancing.

"Thank you," Lorraine replies. "Everything good is enhanced in the Fifth Dimension. Negative emotions and actions are not present or permitted. You all benefit from your association with the Fifth Dimension. Now, for the final step in your activation, Zeke and I will join your circle." Zeke moves between Eric and Leo, and Lorraine comes to stand between me and Renee. The energy of pure love emanates from her and travels to me though our clasped hands.

"Continue to shimmer. We will raise our vibrations together. Zeke will send you images of what Earth can be like if she enters the Fifth Dimension."

The resonance I felt before is harmonizing all of us, connecting us together and to the mound. The ley line passes beneath where Lorraine and I have clasped hands, and energy courses along it.

I start to see images in my mind. At first I don't understand what Zeke is showing us. The picture is of a huge island of trash and plastic in the ocean. That can't be what the Earth will look like in the Fifth Dimension. Then the image changes. The plastic is gone, and dolphins streak and jump past. Huge whales breach the surface in a display of pure joy.

The next scene is of ocean again, but this time it's an iceberg that I see: one lone block of ice in a vast ocean. On the iceberg is an emaciated polar bear. In the next image, the water is full of floating ice and large icebergs. The polar bear is on one of the icebergs. She is huge and well fed. She is accompanied by two smaller adolescent bears. More images flash through my head. Flooded coastal cities and those same cities pristine and sparkling. Burnt-out forests and those same forests lush, green, and teeming with wildlife. Clear-cut forests in the Amazon and then beautiful rainforests. Strip mining operations replaced by wild mountainous regions.

I see images of bombs dropped from planes onto cities and exploding on the ground, killing countless thousands of people. Then I see what looks like a huge outdoor party where people of every race and creed are celebrating together, dancing and laughing. The next before image shows filthy cities, trash blowing, buildings covered in graffiti, gangs roaming freely through the streets. In smaller towns it isn't quite as bad, but no one is outside and there is a general feeling of fear and despair.

The new Earth image shows a striking difference. The cities and towns are a true melting pot of cultures and races all living together with respect for their differences and acknowledgment of their many similarities. Zeke shows us libraries like the one we saw on Arcturus and the stream of Collective Consciousness swirling through it all. The overall impression is one of peace and harmony and prosperity. I also see many translucent orbs floating through the air, just like I saw on Arcturus, and I imagine these are also beings not in physical form.

Then he shows us volcanoes erupting, spewing ash into the air, lava destroying everything in its path. He shows us earthquakes causing terrific loss of life and terrible damage to buildings and bridges and homes, triggering tsunami waves that do equal damage. Then the images stop.

Zeke begins chanting in a language I don't understand, but I get an impression of what the words mean. He is offering up prayers for Earth and humanity, praying that we can change the path we are on and care for Gaia, our Earth home, and ascend to the Fifth Dimension. The notes of his song move through and around me, and I imagine it flowing all around the others gathered on top of the mound. When he finishes, we're all quiet for a few minutes. Then Lorraine speaks.

"You may have recognized that many of the images of Earth that Zeke showed us are already happening today. Clear cutting, strip mining, and crime-ridden portions of cities. Earth and her human inhabitants are already going down the path of destruction, all due to the actions of humans. You are part of the solution, as are many other Light Workers who will be doing similar work. Share the message that Earth can only absorb so much abuse before cataclysmic results occur. That there is a purpose and meaning to life, which people are either knowingly or unknowingly searching for. You are part of the solution, reaching one person at a time. Now we will activate the four of you and the ley line of Angel Mound.

"Everyone move to the center of the circle where the crystal is placed," Lorraine instructs us.

Whereas before she was a few inches taller than me, now she towers over me by more than a foot. She shines with an inner beauty that's hard to even describe. It's less about how she appears and more about who she is. She places her hand over the crystal and the rest of us follow suit. Zeke's hand is on top.

"Repeat after me." Lorraine speaks in the same language Zeke did. Although I've never heard it before and don't understand the words, I know what she's saying. She's clearing away old blockages from the ley line and opening it up to connect with the other ley lines that link sacred sites all over the Earth.

As I speak the words after her, their meaning becomes clear. A cool wave flows through me from head to toe, washing away negative emotions and leaving behind a clarity of purpose. I'm lifted up to a higher vibration, a higher level of consciousness.

I feel the earth trembling under my feet and think we're in for another earthquake, but instead there's a great flash of light and heat from beneath our hands. I instinctively pull my hand away from the heat and am immediately horrified that I may have broken the connection.

"It is done," Lorraine says. "Both the mound and all of you are activated. It's time for Zeke and me to leave you. Remember, as with the other Ascended Masters and teachers you met, we are never more than a thought away. Blessings to you in all of your endeavors."

I run over to her, tears streaming down my face, and hug first her, then Zeke. This sparks off hugging and tears all around.

Finally, after everyone has been hugged, Lorraine says, "We will leave you now in form, but not in spirit." And they slowly dissolve into thin air.

I look at the spot where I had placed the crystal on the ground, but now there's nothing but charred grass. I sit down on the grass and lean back on my elbows, looking up at the sky. Leo lies down next to me and looks up too.

"Hard to believe we were up there," he says. "Zeke and Lorraine are somewhere up there now."

"Yeah. It makes me wonder what other beings and life forms are out there that we don't know about. I wish we could travel to more places. Having had the experience, it's hard not to want more," I say.

"I feel the same way," Eric says. "We know so much more than we did before, but it's still hardly anything compared to what's out there. You know, we can see Arcturus in the southeastern sky. It's the fourth brightest star visible from Earth." He's silent for a moment. "I think that's it there."

I look in the direction he's pointing. A bright, reddish-gold star seems to hover over the horizon. Arcturus. Maybe I'll travel there again someday. I'm glad I can see it with my naked eye. I can be reminded about what happened these past few weeks whenever I see it.

I look down at Leo lying beside me. "What are you thinking?"

"That my whole worldview has changed. The things I thought were true aren't, and what is true is literally out of this world. It's going to take me a while to adjust." He moves his arms behind his head and rests his head on his hands.

I brush his hair back from his forehead. "Me too." I'm no longer worried about what will happen between me and Leo when we go back to our regular lives. I know we'll stay together.

For a while no one says anything, each lost in our own thoughts. Leo traces circles on my knee, making me shiver.

"Look!" Renee points to the west, where a shooting star blazes across the sky. "Make a wish!"

My wish is that I'll know what to do and how to do it going forward.

"So what now?" Eric asks. "We've been doing all of this crazy stuff the past few weeks, but what are we supposed to do next?"

"I think we're still going to be experiencing the world in a different way," Renee says. "With more awareness and connectedness." She places her hands on the ground behind her and leans back. "This has changed me. I'm planning to continue with the shimmering and meditation practice. I think it's more of a beginning than an ending."

"You're right, I feel changed too," I reply. "I guess it's just that . . . while I've changed, the world has stayed the same. Now we have to think about how to go about the mission—telling other people."

Just as I finish speaking, someone approaches from the path around the mound and calls out. It's Scott with Lainey.

"Hey, I should have known we'd find you guys up here," Scott says. "We saw a flash of light from down at the campfire and came to see what's going on. What are you guys doing? Also, what's the deal with Zeke and Lorraine? Have you heard anything about what happened to them?"

I sit up and brush bits of dirt and grass from my hands. "Well, if you have a few minutes, sit down, and we'll tell you all about it."

And so it begins.

Acknowledgments

Writing a novel is never done in a vacuum, and I rely heavily on others in doing my research, story development, and editing (especially editing—I'm a terrible speller, and my punctuation is not always stellar!). I'd like to thank some of the people who helped me along the way in creating and completing *Catalyst*.

Thank you to the archaeologists at Strawtown Koteewi Park and Indiana University's anthropology department for helping me understand archaeology and visit actual dig sites. I also visited Angel Mounds archaeology site in southern Indiana and Cahokia Mounds Native American site outside of St. Louis for information and inspiration on the mound-building civilizations. All their information was extremely useful and accurate. Any errors in the book are entirely mine. I also took poetic license and morphed the actual sites into a fictional site for the archaeological dig in the novel.

Thank you to David K. Miller and his series of books on connecting to the Arcturians. I got a great deal of information for Zeke and Lorraine from his books and found them to be fascinating and enlightening.

My writer's group was extremely helpful in the revision process. I rewrote the first chapter half a dozen times before I got it right following their excellent advice. Mindy Baker, Cindy Argentine, and Brian Schmidt provided invaluable feedback and suggestions.

My editor extraordinaire, Erynn Newman, who cleaned up and tightened up my prose and gave great feedback on character and plot development.

My son, Alex Katsaropoulos, who created an amazing cover and provided feedback on the manuscript and constant support and encouragement. Marcie is a lot less strident thanks to his input!

My daughter, Katie Katsaropoulos, who came to the rescue at the last minute and provided constant love and support.

My brothers, Mark and Rob Richardson, who read the first (terrible) draft and bravely told me that it didn't work and what I needed to change. (And I bravely listened!)

My boyfriend, Keith Knostman, for reading the manuscript and providing valuable feedback, for encouraging and supporting me, schlepping me and my stuff all over the Midwest on the book tour for *The Field*, and sharing the adventure. And, most importantly, for your love.

And to Tom Reale, president and COO of Brown Books Publishing, and the entire team at Brown Books, for completely "getting" my books and for getting them out in the world.

I couldn't have done it without all of you.

About the Author

Tracy Richardson wasn't always a writer, but she was always a reader. Her favorite book growing up was *A Wrinkle in Time* by Madeleine L'Engle. In a weird way that book even shaped her life through odd synchronicities. She has a degree in biology like Mrs. Murry, and, without realizing it, she named her children Alex and Katie after Meg's parents!

Tracy uses her science background in her writing through her emphasis on environment issues and metaphysics. When she's not writing you'll find her doing any number of creative activities—painting furniture, knitting sweaters, or cooking up something in the kitchen. Tracy lives in Indianapolis.